THE ALAMO

"Remember the Alamo!"

A flaming war cry from American history.

Remember 185 ragged volunteers who defied an army of 7,000 disciplined troops.

Remember Colonel David Crockett, Jim Bowie and Colonel Bill Travis and their men who defended a ruined mission called the Alamo for almost two weeks until the last man fell, cut down at his post.

What they did makes a truly magnificent tale, superbly recounted by Steve Frazee, who has caught the savage immediacy of John Wayne's great motion picture, *The Alamo*.

Steve Frazee was born in Salida, Colorado, and for the decade 1926–1936 he worked in heavy construction and mining in his native state. He also managed to pay his way through Western State College in Gunnison, Colorado, from which in 1937 he graduated with a bachelor's degree in journalism. The same year he also married. He began making major contributions to the Western pulp magazines with stories set in the American West as well as a number of North-Western tales published in *Adventure*. Few can match his Western novels which are notable for their evocative, lyrical descriptions of the open range and the awesome power of natural forces and their effects on human efforts. *Cry Coyote* (1955) is memorable for its strong female protagonists who actually influence most of the major events and bring about the resolution of the central conflict in this story of wheat growers and expansionist cattlemen. *High Cage* (1957) concerns five miners and a woman snowbound at an isolated gold mine on top of Bulmer Peak in which the twin themes of the lust for gold and the struggle against the savagery of both the elements and human nature interplay with increasing, almost tormented intensity. *Bragg's Fancy Woman* (1966) concerns a free-spirited woman who is able to tame a family of thieves. *Rendezvous* (1958) ranks as one of the finest mountain man books and *The Way Through the Mountains* (1972) is a major historical novel. Not surprisingly, many of Frazee's novels have become major motion pictures. According to the second edition of *Twentieth Century Western Writers*, a Frazee story is possessed of 'flawless characterization, particularly when it involves the clash of human passions; believable dialogue; and the ability to create and sustain damp-palmed suspense.' His latest Western novel is *Hidden Gold* (1997).

THE ALAMO

Steve Frazee

GUNSMOKE

This hardback edition 2002
by Chivers Press
by arrangement with
Golden West Literary Agency

ISBN 0 7540 8178 8

British Library Cataloguing in Publication Data available.

Printed and bound in Great Britain by
BOOKCRAFT, Midsomer Norton, Somerset

To John Wayne
who has helped to perpetuate
The Alamo as an international
symbol of man's undying
fight for dignity and
freedom

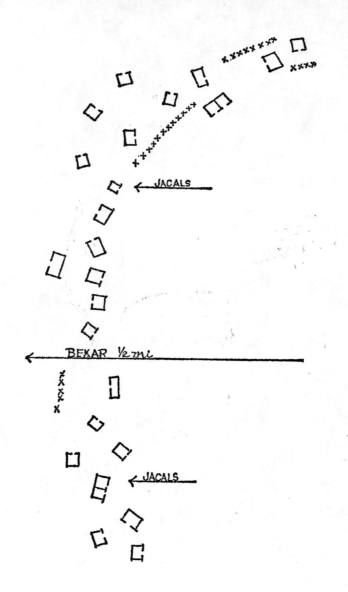

JACALS

BEXAR ½ mi.

JACALS

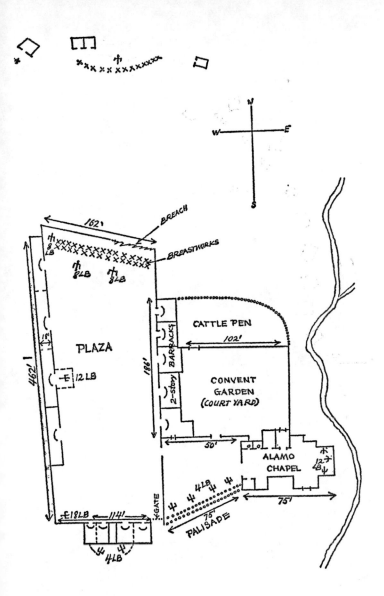

"No one book can be expected to encompass the vast canvas of John Wayne's "The Alamo," but Steve Frazee has turned out a masterpiece!"
—James Edward Grant

CHAPTER 1

THE MORNING sun warmed the old bones of Veedor Bustamente as he took his usual place on the bench on the eastern
side of the cantina in San Antonio de Bexar, there to wait
breakfast, which would be brought in time by one of the children
of his worthless grandson, Gonzalo, who now owned the
cantina.

Big of belly and of mouth was Gonzalo, who was good
only for making children and screaming loudly when the wine
was spilled by careless hands. Veedor grunted with contempt
for the world of men in general. He drew his serape across
his chest. He waited. For the old there was nothing but waiting left.

Across the river, the crumbling mission of the Alamo took
a newness from the thin sunlight. It was always that way in
early morning, before the harshness fell upon the long grass-
lands around Bexar and the mission many years deserted by
the Franciscans.

Only in early morning could a *viejo*, an old man, dream of
days of the long shout when everything was young and men
were great.

Where were the great ones now? Dead of Apache arrows,
dead of the fierce Comanche lance, dead of revolutions that
promised much and turned to ashes; and a few of them had
died of the *coraje*, the loneliness that turns into wildness until
a man must kill or be killed. Of all the old ones, the great
ones, of Veedor's youth, only Amador de Leon had died in
bed, which had been a monstrous disgrace that he felt keenly.

And so will I, thought Veedor, absolved by a priest who
will wonder why I laugh.

He dozed, waiting for his breakfast. Waiting. His teeth
were still strong. His hair was thick and white, and his hawkish old face bore a startling resemblance even in repose to the
captain of Cortez who was his ancestor.

9

He roused when someone touched his knee several times and called his name. "Do not shake me apart," Veedor grumbled. "I do not sleep."

"Yes, Grandfather," said Bernal. In one brown fist he held frijoles wrapped in a tortilla.

"Always noisy, always disturbing one." Veedor took the food. Of all the children of his worthless grandson, Bernal showed promise. He was wide and strong, of twelve years, and sometimes he would stay to listen to tales of the old great days. And he never came with half the frijoles spilled from the tortilla because of careless haste to bring an old man's breakfast and be gone.

"More of the North Americans left last night," Bernal said. "Some of them stole horses to go."

Veedor chewed his beans. It was always like that after a battle. The victors grew tired of victory, lonely for their women, and so they went home.

"It was a great battle, was it not?" Bernal asked.

"When they took Bexar? It was nothing."

Bernal still had great respect for the opinion of the old one, although he knew that Veedor, because of anger over being kept inside during the days of fighting, had slept through most of the battle.

"Noisy children firing muskets and shouting," Veedor said, eating with relish. "General Cos was a coward to give up the town." He spat out a hard bean. "And he is a brother-in-law of Santa Anna, which is worse than being a coward."

Now the North Americans were beginning to rouse. They roosted any place, those men. They made much of coming from sleep, yawning, shouting at each other, using anyone's wood to make their fires.

As usual, some of them were coming to the cantina for breakfast.

Buckskin men who carried their long rifles wherever they went, who walked with springy stride, with pistols and long knives in their belts. Drink and women were much on their minds, and they talked forever, like politicians. Among them, too, were Mexicans who had no love for Santa Anna, who was now ruler of all Mexico.

These were the men who had taken Bexar, and now they were here and they didn't know what to do with their victory. To begin, they had allowed General Cos and his men to go free after their surrender. That was not the proper way of

10

war. If the enemy wished to surrender, that was good. It kept you from losing more men, but after the enemy surrendered you were obliged to kill him.

Had not the Spanish taught that lesson long ago, and before the Spanish the Aztecs?

A group of the North Americans greeted Veedor courteously in passing. They all knew him. He nodded in return, his dark old eyes wise with knowing what kind of men they were. Now that breakfast was settling well within his stomach, he could admit, with certain reservations, that all the great ones were not dead.

These North Americans, whose tongue he understood far better than they knew, bore the mark of the long winds on the *llano*. They spoke with a strange drawl, mixing Mexican and French into their talk, and Veedor knew that most of them still staying in Bexar were not settlers from the land of Texas but men from across the Mississippi who had come to a fight for reasons that could not be understood, just as Veedor and Amador de Leon had rushed to fights in the old days when some ragged mestizo rode into camp crying, "Liberty!"

And what was liberty? A chance to die in bed.

Veedor belched. He eyed Bernal, who was twisting his bare feet on the hard-packed earth, anxious to go into the cantina and mingle with the North Americans. "What other news do you bring this morning?"

"Santa Anna is coming with his army."

"That is to be expected."

"The North American commander has sent messengers to Goliad, and elsewhere. He seeks advice. He does not know what to do, and his men are leaving."

"That is understandable." Veedor looked across at the Alamo. By the creep of sun along the west wall of the chapel he could tell when it was time to move to the shady side of the cantina. "Do they talk of staying, of going to the mission?"

Bernal shrugged. "They talk, but no one knows."

"It is not a place to defend."

"Yes, Grandfather."

"The place to fight is where there is openness, where you can ride away quickly if all does not go well. You must understand this. When I fought Comanches . . ." Veedor began his story, but the breakfast was good and the sun was good, and soon he dozed.

When he roused to continue, Bernal was gone.

11

He watched riders coming through the brown grass to the east. More buckskin men with haste. They rode well, those long-legged ones, on tough mustangs, carrying their rifles in Comanche cases. When they drummed past the cantina and went toward the house where the North American commander lived, Veedor knew that he had not seen them before, but like the others, they bore the mark of the *llano*.

That was his way of grading men, though they might never have seen a true *llano*, a great open plain where the grass whispered high and Comanches appeared from nowhere. But men of a certain stamp carried that mark, in their bearing, in the eyes, in the way they turned their heads with quickness when danger threatened.

They were men, yes, perhaps not of the greatness of those of Veedor's time, but strong ones just the same.

He raised his eyes once more to the old mission across the river. A fort, a *presidio*. It was to laugh! The North Americans who had fought from house to house during the taking of Bexar would never pen themselves in that place if there was more fighting.

Already blood-touched was the Alamo. The year after Veedor grew too old to be a soldier, in 1810, the garrison of the Alamo had shouted liberty in the name of the priest Hidalgo, who led the revolution at that time.

For allowing such a thing to happen the commander of the Alamo had been killed by the Spanish lords of Mexico and some of the officers had been dragged, without ceremony, to their deaths by wild mustangs.

Only two years later the man called Kemper, leading North American bandits and Mexican republicans, who were also bandits, had stormed the Alamo during another revolution. Veedor shook his head at the stupidity of North Americans.

They had let the garrison leave with honor, but some of the Mexican leaders of Kemper's force understood war, and they had taken the soldiers a few miles from Bexar and cut their throats to a man. And this Veedor had seen himself, and though it had not been the most pleasant of sights on that sunny day beside the little pond, he knew that it was necessary.

No, it was not well to march out of a fort in surrender, which he would have told Bernal, if the boy had stayed to listen.

Inside the cantina there was much laughter, the deep voices
12

of the North Americans, and Bernal's delighted squeal, and the shrill cackling of Serafina Hernandez and others who were much at the cantina these days. And that whore of all whores himself, Gonzalo, was saying, "Yes, yes, gentlemen!" and making himself agreeable, if such a thing could be.

Did he not know that the North Americans trusted him no farther than one might throw a wild bull, as indeed they could trust no one in Bexar but themselves? It was the way of things. In Bexar were many people who hated Santa Anna, that man of scorpion eyes and pale face who looked like he had read too many books by poor candlelight. Of a certainty, many Mexicans in Bexar would like to cut his throat, including Veedor Bustamente, who hated anyone in authority as a matter of lifelong habit.

But if Santa Anna came to Bexar with his army, hate would become love, until he left again. Did not Gonzalo, the wine belly, the pig, know this even as he begged the favor of the North Americans? No man in Bexar could be an open friend of theirs if Santa Anna came.

And he would come. Veedor doubted not the intelligence supplied by Bernal. By day and by night lean, tough mestizos entered Bexar from the blistered deserts to the south, from Goliad and Refugio, and from beyond the Sabine. They knew what they had seen, and they left by day and night, couriers speeding to and from Santa Anna.

Two of them were lying now, as if in sleep, under the big tree beyond the entrance to the cantina, their sombreros over their faces—and their ears dragging the ground. Veedor shrugged. It was the way of things.

Half drowsing, but still with part of his mind seeing sharp impressions, Veedor watched the morning stir. Lares drove his pigs to their pen near the river, where they could wallow in the mud until evening, when he would turn them out again to root for scraps in the village.

He watched women taking their washing to the river. Teresa Pineda was with child again. When was she not? Who was it this time, Juan Sedeno? He would ask Bernal.

Two more North Americans burst from the trees, riding around the women. The riders turned to look back and one of them laughed. As they passed the shop of Escalante the maker of boots, the tall one, dark as an Indian, asked, "What's that thing across the river, Cahill?"

"The Alamo mission."

13

"Missions! Is that all you got down here?"

Now the sun was beginning to reach down a little on the distant chapel wall, almost to the large place where plaster had fallen away years before.

Veedor's father had been one of the garrison of Indian fighters who had given the mission *presidio* its name. Long ago, when coming from the Pueblo de San Carlos del Alamo de Parras, with the simplicity of soldiers they had called their new post the Alamo.

Ah, they were men in those days!

Veedor himself had been a soldier of dragoons, fighting Indians, the Spanish, his own people, and again the Spanish; but it was the wild, free days on the *llano*, long before he was a soldier, that he remembered best.

On memories of those times he dozed, sleeping past time to change his seat to the shade, which was of no moment, since it was mainly habit anyway, and the day was not too warm.

Great shouting roused him. Riders were coming into Bexar and others were running their horses out to greet them. In the midst of the new arrivals Veedor saw a man known to everyone in Bexar, a man who, though wealthy with large holdings along the San Antonio, was still of the people.

Jim Bowie.

With pride Veedor watched him. The fairness of the sun was in Bowie's face, the copper of the Aztecs in his hair. He sat his saddle like a giant, like the great ones of Veedor's time.

This was a man.

The riders turned at the saddlery but Bowie swung from them and came toward the cantina. The people of Bexar, whose liking of North Americans had been sadly strained, watched Bowie with affection. He was as close to them as any North American could be, and in spite of the reputation of his terrible knife, he was not one to cause trouble for reasons of no importance.

And this was much to say of any North American.

Like most *tejanos*, Big Jim was a citizen of Mexico and of the church, although that last fact troubled him no more than it did many of the saints of Bexar who were well known in the cantinas.

Big Jim's wife had been of Bexar too, a beautiful woman, daughter of Veramendi, Lieutenant-Governor of Coahuila-

Texas. She too had been loved by the people of Bexar. Three years before she had died of cholera, and with her the two Bowie children, her father and mother and other members of her family.

Deeply had the people mourned the loss, and they had understood why Big Jim had gone away for a long time, and they understood, too, why he now sometimes drank like a *ladron* of the Sabine who had made a great haul of booty.

Straight to the cantina of Gonzalo he came, and those inside rushed to the doorway and called for him to join them, but he smiled and said, "I'll see you later, boys."

Then to Veedor he spoke, bowing a little in the saddle. "How goes it, Don Bustamente?"

The smile that Veedor gave was thin upon his lips but it reached deep into his heart, for he was greatly honored. "There is sun, and a friend speaks. What more could an old one ask?"

"The oldness is only in your face, but not in your eyes and heart, Don Bustamente." Big Jim smiled and gave Veedor a Comanche salute and then rode on toward the house of the North American commandante.

It was good. Veedor felt younger. He sat straighter and forgot for a time his poor legs. With the keenness of a hawk he watched the two mestizos rise and yawn and make a great pretense of having been asleep, and then they went to their horses with the clumsy walk of those who are horsemen.

Bernal came later, full of news. "Those with Big Jim say he comes from General Houston to destroy the Alamo and—"

"You are filled with gossip. You should wash clothing with the women at the river."

Hurt, Bernal started to turn away.

"Wait," said Veedor. "I have something to say." He tried to compose himself to give weight and dignity to his announcement. "Big Jim is a *cristiano,* it is true, and he was not born of us, but still I have decided that he is one of the great ones."

A sudden stillness came to Bernal's brown features. He had never understood just what the old one meant by his frequent references to the great ones, but now he caught a glimpse of the meaning in the fierce, hawkish, withered face of his great-grandfather, and he felt without knowing, this young Bernal, how terrible it must be to grow very old and have

15

broken knees and be worth no more than a bench in the morning sun and a shady place when the day grew hot.

"Remember well what I have said," Veedor admonished sternly.

Bernal nodded hastily, and then he ran back to see what Big Jim and the other late arrivals were doing.

And now the sun was high on the ancient chapel of the Alamo. The date was January 19, 1836.

CHAPTER 2

COLONEL JOSEPH C. NEILL, Army of Texas, commandancy of Bexar, which included the Alamo and environs, sprawled in his leather chair in an unmilitary manner as he listened to Jim Bowie's report of conditions in Texas.

"There's not a Mexican garrison left, but neither is there much interest in keeping it that way." Bowie tasted the commander's whiskey and made a face. "You *are* down to short rations, Colonel."

Neill cut his hand through the air in a disgusted gesture. "No money, men, provisions—not even a definite order from anyone I can trust. I'm just sitting here."

"As I was saying, Colonel, there's no Mexican troops left in Texas, and not much of a Texas army either. Colonel Fannin has what there is at Goliad. I've been to Copano, San Felipe, Goliad, here last month, as you know, and back to San Felipe, trying to recruit." Bowie shook his head. "There's not much interest in fighting. Most people think we've already won and now they're talking of making some kind of peaceful settlement with the Mexican government."

"With Santa Anna? Hell!" Neill rose and walked to the doorway. Three of his volunteers were staggering down the street, one of them trailing his rifle stock in the dust behind him.

They glanced at Neill and one of them pawed the air near his shoulder in a sort of salute. "Hi ya, Colonel!" he said amiably. "What kind of news has Bowie got?"

Colonel Neill stared the man down. The volunteer grinned sheepishly and said, "Just asking, Colonel. Hell, we're all

16

friends here, ain't we?" He lurched on to join his two companions.

Without turning from the doorway Neill said, "I've got about one hundred men here, damn' little powder and damn' little of anything else, but I say this is the place to fight." He swung around suddenly, his face dark and angry. "I don't care what the talk is back east, the San Antonio River is our natural line of defense, from here to Goliad. What do you think, Colonel Bowie?"

There it was, that title of colonel again. Bowie stared at the table a moment before pouring himself another drink. It was an unenterprising man indeed who couldn't pick himself up some kind of military title on the frontier, but of late Bowie's title was beginning to hurt.

Of all the people in Texas who had been granted, or helped themselves to, authority, only old Sam Houston seemed to have any faith in Jim Bowie. He had tried like the very devil to get Bowie a commission in the Army of Texas, but the Governor, the Lieutenant-Governor, the council and everyone else who was fighting each other had stood together on one point: beware of Jim Bowie, he plays Mexican politics.

The best they had seen fit to give him was authority to raise volunteers. It was a wonder, he thought dourly, that the council had shown enough sense to make Sam Houston commander of their army, such as it was.

"What's your view?" Neill insisted.

"I can't say if Bexar is the place to fight. Houston doesn't know either. He was inclined to favor blowing up the Alamo and falling back, but still, he said for me to look the situation over and see what I thought." Bowie paused. "What have you heard of the Mexican army?"

"Rumors." Neill spread his hands. "Santa Anna seems to be moving, but that's all we can say. One thing, his whole force will be dragged down from the march, if he does come, and maybe by then we'll have heavy reinforcements. What do you think of the chances that we will?"

Bowie shrugged. "I brought thirty men. You've got one hundred, you say. Right now, that's the army here."

"I had a hundred four yesterday, Colonel. If I could round them up today for a count, it might be seventy-five, or less."

"What would be good garrison strength for the Alamo?"

Neill made a sour face. "A thousand, with all the supplies we'd need to feed them."

17

"Never." Maybe we can scrape up five hundred by sending messengers to every town within a week's ride."

"You think I haven't done that? Half the Army of Texas is riding somewhere trying to recruit the other half. I've asked for orders, I've asked for advice for weeks, and you're the first man who's shown up here from anyone in authority, and——"

"Easy, Colonel," Bowie said, studying Neill's angry, excited features. "To tell you the truth, General Houston hasn't got much authority except what he makes for himself. Texas politics right at the moment are worse than any mess you've ever seen in Washington, but maybe some of us can do something on our own.

"First, I suggest we go look at the Alamo. I'm no soldier, but I've fought an Indian or two in my time, so——"

"Pardon, Colonel Bowie, but it is a matter of importance," a voice said from the doorway, and Francisco Ruiz, mayor of Bexar, stepped inside.

Bowie rose to greet him, remembering to ask about his wife, his brother and his cousins, whom, it developed, were all well and flourishing. Then Bowie said, "Colonel Neill commands here, as you know."

"Pardon," said Ruiz, bowing to Neill, "but I thought this was a matter for our great friend, Jim Bowie."

"What is it?" Neill asked.

Ruiz shrugged apologetically. "The cows of Diego Sandoval. They are poor and of not much value, but still the soldiers insist on eating them. At first, they traded rifles and other articles for them, but now they merely kill the cows and eat them, without talk of payment."

The *alcalde* faced Colonel Neill in speaking, but still his appeal was directed at Bowie.

"Goddamn those Mississippians!" Neill said. "I issued specific orders about appropriating property, but still——"

"With your permission, Colonel Neill," Bowie cut in smoothly. He bowed to the *alcalde*. "Please to give our apologies to Diego Sandoval, and tell him that he will be paid this day for the cows the Americans have eaten."

"Thank you," said the mayor. "I knew it would be so." With fine deference to command, he bowed to Neill and went out.

"*Who's* going to pay for those damn' cows?" Neill asked. "The Army hasn't given me one cent for anything."

"I'll take care of it. Believe me, Colonel Neill, the price of

18

a few cows is a small cost to help keep the good will of the people of Bexar. If we fight here——"

"The good citizens of Bexar will stab us in the back! Don't tell me. I've tried to recruit some of the Mexicans here. They have no use for Santa Anna, but they have less use for us. Bexar swarms with spies, Colonel Bowie. They know what I think before I know myself."

"That's only natural. We too have our own spies."

Neill growled an oath. "And the only ones that can be trusted are white, and sometimes I'm not even sure of them." He began to pace the floor.

Bowie walked to the step outside and leaned against the doorway. Except for Francisco Ruiz, who was staying in the shade as much as possible as he went to find Sandoval, the plaza was deserted. To some, Bexar was a village of mud huts and filth and shiftless people, but Bowie saw far more than that.

He knew the people of Bexar. He understood them, and if they did all that Neill had spoken of, and more, he could still look upon them with understanding. He glanced up the slope to the house where he and Ursula had lived in happiness, the house with the deep, cool windows and heavy walls that had surrounded for a time the one real love he had known.

The old pangs of lostness twisted inside him again. Going back to the United States for a year hadn't helped, and neither had his frantic speculation in land after his return, nor his wild, dangerous—and successful—gambling in Mexican politics. And though drinking eased the pain for a short time, that too was no answer.

Far away in the misty blue mountains of Coahuila she and the children had died of the plague, while he had stayed in Bexar, untouched. Christ, where was the answer to that!

A man could fight anything he could get at with his hands or with a knife, but Bowie's enemy now was a hurt inside him as deadly as the heavy blade against his thigh. Three years and still no forgetting. He stared toward the Coahuila Mountains.

Colonel Neill stopped pacing, caught by the grimness of Bowie's face. Half envious, half irritated, Neill wondered what made Bowie the man he was. It wasn't the size of him, though God knew he was big enough, well over six feet and at least a hundred eighty pounds, with a leanness that spoke of tremendous power, cat-fast.

19

You couldn't say what made a man stand out from all others around him. Not his reputation for quick combat under any circumstances. Not his willingness to gamble against brutal odds. There were frontier toughs by the barge load who would try, and who could do, the things that Jim Bowie had done.

Damn it to hell, thought Neill, there's a gentleness about that man that defies describing, but who the hell out here was ever attracted to gentleness? Perplexed, Neill went back to pacing the floor.

The weight of responsibilities that were too uncertain and maybe too big for him to handle settled once more around him like an angry cloud. For a while it had seemed that Bowie was bringing some hard, straightforward order from General Houston that would settle the question of staying in Bexar, or getting out.

"You say that General Houston has left the decision up to you whether to defend the Alamo or not?" Neill asked.

"He asked me to make a report one way or another."

"All right, let's go look at the damned ruin," Neill said impatiently. "Not that I haven't stalked around it until I'm disgusted with the sight of things."

Bowie nodded but he didn't move. He stared into the tawny distance of the wild land to the south. A fearsome crossing for any army, but he knew Antonio Lopez de Santa Anna Perez de Lebron, and he knew the hard fiber of battle-seasoned Mexican cavalry.

The desert was there, but it wouldn't stop the Mexican army. Sam Houston knew that. Others knew it, but still there were a lot of fools who did not. They were crying liberty and independence for Texas before they had seen any real fighting.

"Let's go look at your mission," Bowie said.

On the way they met Lieutenant Dickerson, a slender, square-jawed man with a hot worry in his eyes. His blue tunic was unbuttoned and sweat was running into the V of his shirt.

"Colonel," he said, with the barest of salutes, "six more men have traded off their rifles for food and whiskey."

"Confine them!"

"Where?"

"Find a place. Make a jail. Christ, man!"

"Yes, sir." Dickerson wiped sweat from his brow with his sleeve. "And how do we feed them in confinement?"

"Let their friends feed them!"

Dickerson nodded. "I'll also have to let their friends tear down any kind of quarters I confine them in. They're Irish, Colonel. If we throw them into any kind of jail, which I doubt we can do, we'll lose a quarter more of the army."

Neill took a deep breath, and as he let it out, the anger came with it and he stood there tired and worried. He glanced at Bowie.

"With the Colonel's permission, I'll try to get the rifles back," Bowie said, "and I'll try to arrange it so no more weapons will be traded."

Neill was relieved and at the same time exasperated. "You're quite a friend of these Mexicans, aren't you?"

"I hope so," Bowie said evenly. "Do you mean any more than that, Colonel Neill?"

He spoke with so little emphasis that Neill was on the verge of a hot reply, but he took a long look into Bowie's Scotch-gray eyes and changed his mind. "I meant no more than what I said," he answered, which could have been construed as no apology at all, a fact which Neill realized.

Bowie took it at face value. "Do I have your permission to see what I can do about the rifles?"

"By all means!" Neill said.

Bowie glanced toward the Alamo. "Then let's forego our inspection of the fort, shall we? We'll have more than enough time to make up our minds about it." He turned and walked back down the street.

Some men made you crawl inside when they backed you down. They pushed and took pride in making you hate yourself for some weakness you could not help. Not Jim Bowie though, the Colonel thought. Bowie let you off with honor because there was no meanness in him.

There was part of the answer Neill hadn't found in his quarters when trying to size up Jim Bowie.

"You think he can get those rifles back without some kind of ruckus?" Lieutenant Dickerson asked.

"I'm sure of it." Neill paused. "You know something, Al, it's early, but I think I'm going to go get drunk. Join me?"

Dickerson grinned. "The next time you ask me, Colonel. The baby's got a touch of summer complaint and Sue is worried. While I can, I think I'll stay with them."

21

Colonel Neill didn't get drunk. He allowed himself to reach the point where his worries no longer seemed so burdensome, and then he wrote dispatches to Henry Smith, the Governor of Texas, an independent state that existed only in the minds of men who called themselves Texans.

Afterward, Neill wondered if he had written to the right man. Such was the wondrous state of Texas politics that the Governor was an impeached man, though refusing to acknowledge the fact.

At dusk Lieutenant Dickerson came in to report that every volunteer who had traded off his weapon now had it back.

"How'd he do it?" Neill asked.

"I didn't bother to inquire." Dickerson smiled. "I'll have a drink now."

"What's Bowie doing?"

"Drinking."

"Here's to him," said Colonel Neill. He wiped his drooping mustache and lifted a glass of rum that had been sitting before him for an hour.

CHAPTER 3

FROM A palisaded earthen platform inside the west wall of the mission, Bowie and Colonel Neill surveyed the half mile of space between them and Bexar.

"They'll occupy the town first, of course," Neill said. "Then they'll come in against this side."

Bowie scratched his chest. "Why will they?"

"Because it's the longest wall where we can't bring angling fire against them. They can mass more men against it than any other part of the fort."

"That's a good way to lose a lot of men," Bowie mused, thinking of riflemen firing from loopholes all along the west wall. But there were no loopholes. Some previous Mexican garrison had built earthen mounds inside the defense, on which sharpshooters could stand.

The wall was between nine and twelve feet high, rock work held with a natural cement, about three feet thick and close to a hundred fifty yards long. Storerooms and barracks lay along almost the entire length of it, giving added strength.

22

As Bowie turned to look east across the mission plaza, he bumped against a cannon, a smoothbore with the muzzle elevated and gathering rust. He looked at it without any particular interest. "How many of these things are there?"

Neill shrugged. "The ordnance officer says we can rustle up maybe fifteen. There's plenty of them here but a lot of them are in bad shape." He added after a pause, "we're short of powder too."

Bowie ran his thumb in a half circle around the rusting muzzle. He reckoned cannon were all right, if you could load them up like a fowling piece and fire them into a jam-pack of humanity; that is, if the humanity didn't pick you off with a rifle first.

"Grant sort of helped himself to supplies here," Neill said.

Bowie grunted. He knew all about Dr. James Grant, who had looted the Alamo of whatever took his fancy when he was planning an expedition to capture the Mexican port of Matamoros. What wasn't the army short of, including men?

He studied the east wall, across the plaza. The northern run of it was even stronger than this side because of a long two-story barracks, part of which was backed further by the walled convent yard. At the extreme southeast corner of the mission sat the chapel, the tallest building of the whole citadel, its windows partly bricked in by some Mexican garrison of former days.

Out from the main door of the church, which faced west, was a fatal gap in the defenses. The southern end of the east wall of the inner plaza was only a few feet high, and from the front of the chapel there was only open ground to the south.

The north and south ends of the rough rectangle that formed the plaza looked sound enough, discounting crumbling places in the top of the masonry.

"I don't know much about cannon," Bowie said, "but that southeast corner sure leaves one hell of a hole to defend."

Neill nodded. "We'll have to build some kind of breastworks there."

With a half grin Bowie looked at the southwest corner of the plaza where a detachment of Texas regulars had been sent an hour before to build firing ramps of earth. None of them were in sight now. Building anything in the Alamo was going to be quite a problem, unless the men saw an immediate need for it.

23

"Maybe we ought to blow things sky-high and light out of here," Bowie suggested.

"No, by God!" Neill slapped the muzzle of the cannon with his hand. "We'll stop Santa Anna here or all of Texas goes under! If we can't stop him, we'll slow him down."

Bowie shrugged. "With a hundred thirty men?"

"We'll have a force," Neill argued. "All of Texas will rally here!"

They walked down the ramp to the plaza. "See those cannon?" the Colonel said, pointing to pieces scattered everywhere in disorder. "We haven't got enough horses and mules to take them if we abandon the Alamo. We haven't even got enough horses to send out scouting parties. The Texas army needs those cannon, Colonel Bowie. I say stay here and keep them."

Neill made a strong point, Bowie admitted. If they destroyed the fort and pulled out, which General Houston had strongly suggested that they do, the Mexican army wouldn't be delayed in any way by the action.

"What do *you* think?" Neill asked.

Bowie took a long look around the plaza. It was a gamble. They could be starved out, or cut down by sickness, or if the Mexicans brought enough men, the small force of Americans could be worn down and overwhelmed by sheer weight. Still, it was a good place to put up a fight, and a good place for Texans to rally to.

Unbidden, another thought came to Bowie's mind: And a good place to die.

He said, "Let's make our fight here, Colonel Neill."

"I knew you'd stand with me!" They started toward the main gate at the southeast corner of the plaza. Suddenly Neill remembered something. "Now where's that work detail?"

"Telling each other lies in the porte-cochere, I imagine," Bowie said dryly.

Neill trotted toward the arched entrance in the south wall, flanked by barracks. He found the detail taking their ease on earth-filled cowhides that partly blocked the south end of the tunnel-like entrance.

"What's this!" Neill shouted. "You men were assigned to a task."

Private Wilson spat against the wall. "We got a mite tired, Colonel."

"Where's Lieutenant Jones?" Neill demanded.

24

Private Cloud grinned. "Some of them fancy New Orleans Greys of his got in trouble with a woman, so he went to see what he could do about it."

"Now *he's* probably in trouble with the woman," said Private Robinson, and the whole detail laughed.

"Don't get so het up, Colonel," Wilson drawled. "Hell, man, nobody's doing no work to speak of, 'specially them miserable volunteers. We ain't seen no Mexican sojers, have we, boys?"

"You will, I'll promise you that!" Neill said. He walked back into the plaza to see Bowie grinning as he stood looking toward the chapel. "Volunteers, regular army—they're all the same. I can't get a lick of work out of them."

"They don't see the need, Colonel. Give 'em time. They'll fight, I'll guarantee that."

Neill stood for a moment gaining control of himself. He shook his head. "I wish I had your easy way of looking at things, Colonel Bowie."

"Do me a favor, don't call me Colonel. I'm a volunteer without any rank at all." A tinge of bitterness touched Bowie's face. "I wish that damned chapel was roofed over and had loopholes near the top."

"I wish a thousand things were done inside this wreck, but what can you do with shiftless men?"

"Easy, Colonel," Bowie said, his voice cool. "These men came here to fight, and they will. Remember that."

They mounted their horses and rode back toward Bexar, past the collection of poor huts on the east side of the river. "There's another thing," Neill said moodily, looking at the shacks, "those *jacals* ought to be razed to the ground."

Bowie glanced at the huts and made no comment.

They turned below the footbridge to ford the river, and it was then that Deaf Smith intercepted them, coming out of the cottonwoods from a fire where five men were roasting meat.

A squat and burly man who had out-foxed Comanches and Apaches ever since he'd been in Texas, Smith was one of the few scouts that Neill trusted implicitly, in spite of the fact that he had once mistaken bundles of forage on a Mexican army packtrain for panniers of pesos.

"Need a horse, Colonel," Smith said.

Neill reined in and sighed. "What happened to yours?"

"Bad leg."

"Have you asked Captain—"

"I'll get him one," Bowie said.

25

"Good one," Smith said.

Bowie nodded. "Bet on that."

The scout tipped his wide-brimmed hat forward and turned to go back to the fire. "Where'd that meat come from?" Neill asked.

"Beef," said Smith, and walked on.

Neill gave Bowie an outraged look, and then, slowly, the Colonel grinned, shaking his head.

Two *carretas*, loaded to the limit with household goods, with pigs and goats in crates, and with solemn, brown-faced children atop the jolting cargo, were entering the ford from the west side. The two riders sat their horses and watched the rough conveyances bump across the stream.

Bowie raised his hand to the drivers. "Go with God."

"They're running away already!" Neill said. "Ask them what they know."

"They know what we know—Santa Anna is on his way. You'll see quite an exodus in the next few days, Colonel."

When Neill reached his quarters, he sent Lieutenant Dickerson to find Lieutenant Jones, with an order for Jones to go back immediately to the work detail he had deserted in the Alamo. After an hour Dickerson reported back. "I can't find him. He must be holed up somewhere."

"Then send another officer over there!"

"No use. The work detail left right after you and Bowie came back."

"Christ, what an army!" Neill cried.

"Anything more, Colonel?"

"Yes! Go get drunk like the volunteers."

Dickerson grinned and went out, back to his family.

Neill flung his coat on a bench. He sat down and began to compose a letter. It occurred to him that Bowie had taken the devil's own time in coming to a decision, since today's inspection of the fort was about the sixth time in the last two weeks that they'd gone over the Alamo; but now—at last—they knew what they were going to do.

That night in his own quarters on the Main Plaza, with Ham, his young Negro servant, watching him quietly, Jim Bowie was also writing to Governor Smith.

"*. . . The salvation of Texas depends in great measure on keeping Bexar out of the hands of the enemy . . . if it was in possession of Santa Anna, there is no stronghold from*

26

which to repel him in his march to the Sabine. Colonel Neill and myself have come to the solemn resolution that we would rather die in these ditches than give them up to the enemy. . . ."

A fandango was in full swing outside, men in buckskin and ragged uniforms whooping as they pranced before Mexican women in swirling skirts. The Texas army in Bexar was enjoying itself to the fullest, and if Santa Anna was coming, by Jem, who had seen him? Time enough to worry when the old bag of whey showed up, if he ever did. Like as not the rumors about him marching north were all Mexican lies.

Young Bernal, who had slipped away from chores at the cantina, watched with delight the cavorting of the funny North Americans. They stomped about imitating bears. They laughed. They leaped high and howled, kicking their heels together. They spun knives and caught them by the handle easily, all the while making violence with their feet.

And in the cantina Gonzalo muttered curses because his son was not there to help. It was getting harder and harder to get money from the North Americans for what they drank. The sad fact was, their money was almost gone. Now it was a good time for the Mexican army to come, with silver that was hard and good to feel in the fingers.

Yet, if the soldiers had been paid, they might drink up everything, and it was a fact that those who kept cantinas often received no sympathy from the officers, and sometimes soldiers were killed, too, before paying what they owed.

No one knew how difficult was the life of an honest cantina owner.

On the top of the still warm stove in the house of his grandson, Veedor Bustamente slept the deep sleep of the aged. Now and then the shouting came to him as if from a great distance across the golden suns of *llanos* he had ridden long ago. Sometimes he groaned as his old knees, shattered in a fall from a *bayo* coyote years before, ached like hot needles were working in the joints.

Watching the fandango in the plaza, Francisco Ruiz, the mayor, moved quietly up behind Alvaro Yanez when he saw the dangerous tension of the man. "Act not with haste, my son. They are visitors."

"And she is my woman!" Yanez muttered, his eyes glitter-

27

ing. "And see how she looks at that large one with the sombrero of fur, and how he holds her."

"It is nothing. In time they will go."

"In time! In the time you speak of, *alcalde*, there will be a child with a great, wide nose and eyes like the sky. Do not speak of time to me."

"Would it be better if the soldiers of Santa Anna were here?"

Yanez sighed helplessly. "Grace of God, no! It will be worse then."

Through the night, out of the desert to the south, came tough mustang ponies bearing lithe, tough riders who had been to the Rio Grande, couriers returned to observe for a time the actions of the pitifully small force of North Americans who called themselves an army.

The day was February 2, 1836.

CHAPTER 4

WHEN LIEUTENANT-COLONEL William Travis rode into Bexar at the head of thirty men, he cast a critical eye on volunteers resting themselves in the sun and he wished most fervently that he could have avoided this assignment. A miserable outpost garrisoned by slouching men who merely paused in their yarning to watch him curiously, not even bothering to rise.

God knew he had tried to avoid coming to Bexar. There was no glory here and he would be only a subordinate. "Take all the men you can rustle and go down there and give Neill a hand," Governor Smith had ordered him. "All I've been getting from Bexar is one message after another asking for reinforcements."

On his way into town Travis had observed that the Alamo wasn't even occupied. What the hell had Bowie and Neill been doing anyway? Another glance at the volunteers was answer enough.

Buck Travis was twenty-seven, a lawyer by profession, an amateur revolutionist by choice. He was a straight, lean six feet in his Texas-blue uniform, a full-lipped man with flashing blue eyes. Maturity was hovering around his face uncertainly.

From his post under a tree near the cantina, a position not

28

assigned, but eminently satisfactory to'him, Private John Mc-Gregor, of Scotland, and lately of Alabama, inquired of his companions, "Noo who's the handsome laddy with the clean shirt?"

Private James Rose of Nacogdoches was removing remnants of Diego Sandoval's last missing cow from his teeth with an Arkansas toothpick. "That's Buck Travis. I remember him in 'thirty-two at Nacogdoches when we took the garrison."

"Hell, he was right here at Bexar when we took it last December," Private Charlie Haskell said. "He'll fight, that one."

"Bless him," said McGregor. "He can have all my fighting too. If I had a horse I'd go back to the sea and swim all the way to New Orleans."

On Soledad Street, Jim Bowie stepped out of the *alcalde's* house when he heard the tramp of horses. He had made no headway whatsoever in recruiting active Mexican support for the defense of the Alamo, which was exactly as he had known it would be, but he was still doing his best to keep the goodwill of the citizens of Bexar, in spite of the army's inroads on everything that was eatable and everything that was chaseable.

Above a low adobe wall he watched the reinforcements arrive at Neill's headquarters, observing that they had brought no more than themselves and whatever they could attach handily to their saddles. He stepped over the wall and went to greet Buck Travis. It was like old Buck to bring his whole force right up to headquarters, instead of dismissing them at the edge of town.

Neill was saying, "You don't know how glad I am to see you, Colonel Travis! How many more are coming?"

"I don't know. No one knows. Have you had any truly reliable reports that Santa Anna is coming?"

Bowie stepped inside, "He'll be here, sooner or later."

"Jim!" Travis cried, and shook hands warmly.

Neill got out a bottle of whiskey and they settled down to discuss the situation, with Travis doing most of the talking. "General Houston has gone on leave to talk to the Cherokees. No one knows who the hell is in authority, so I'm sticking with the Governor, even though he's been impeached."

"What's happening to the Matamoros Expedition?" Neill asked.

Travis shook his head. "God only knows."

"Where can we get reinforcements?"

29

"From Colonel Fannin at Goliad. He's got the biggest force left intact in Texas. I'll write him—I beg your pardon, Colonel, I suggest you write him at once."

Great writers, all of them, including himself, Bowie thought with amusement. He listened in silence to Travis' remarks about establishing discipline among the men at Bexar.

"I've tried," Neill said gloomily.

"It can be done!" Travis said positively.

Like hell, thought Bowie. Firebrand and fighter though he was, Travis just didn't understand long hunters and filibusters—in fact, no one not in his social class. The men of the Bexar garrison were the damnedest fighters in the world, in their individual ways—and the biggest loafers in the world when there was no fighting.

Bowie, Travis, Neill—or General Sam Houston himself was not going to change certain basic characteristics of the volunteers and four-months men who were staying in Bexar, many of them for the simple reason that they had no way to leave.

Let Travis find out for himself.

Travis did find out. He spurred Colonel Neill into holding musters and drills. A West Point graduate among the officers tried valiantly to instill a few military principles into the men. For a day or two some of the regulars went through the motions halfheartedly.

The volunteers observed the drill for a short time and then they went right back to attending rooster fights, trying to make headway with the belles of Bexar and finding drink and food.

Work details sent to the Alamo to strengthen the defenses wound up chasing chickens in the fields between the west wall and the river, or gambling in some of the empty *jacals* or sleeping off the night before on mattresses in one of the storerooms in the fort.

"By God, I never saw such an army!" Travis cried one day in the plaza of the Alamo, where he and Bowie had gone to inspect the progress that a work detail was supposed to be making on the knocking of loopholes in the north wall.

They found a sergeant making himself a pot of coffee. The north wall had not been scratched.

"What happened to your men?" Travis demanded.

30

The sergeant rose from his fire and scratched the back of his neck, and then his rump. "They done left."

"Why did you permit it?"

The sergeant scratched his belly. "It's like this, Colonel, that's a pretty thick wall. They looked it over and some of them thought maybe it wouldn't be so thick from the other side, so they all went over to see.

"That's when I started making the coffee. When I didn't hear any pecking on the other side, I took a look for myself." The sergeant shrugged. "All gone."

Bowie turned away, grinning.

Travis was white in the face. "Do you realize, Sergeant, that you could be court-martialed for this?"

"What's that, Colonel?"

Before Travis could answer, Bowie cut in. "Easy, Buck. You're not dealing with European soldiers. When these men fight they fight, and when they rest they take real hound-dog ease."

"That's just what I was thinking!" the sergeant said, and scratched his armpits vigorously.

On the chilly evening of February 10, Colonel Neill called Travis and Bowie to his quarters. Neill rubbed his hands as he paced the floor. "I've received news that my family is ill. I'm relieving myself as commander of this garrison to go home for a few days. Colonel Travis, you will succeed me here in command. I've had the order written and it will be posted tomorrow."

Bowie saw the quick glow of elation that came to Travis' face. He trusted the man, but he knew how hot-headed he was, and how much he had irritated the men of the garrison by trying to enforce discipline. The change of command wasn't going to set well with the men, and that was a fact.

"You understand, of course, Jim?" Neill asked, and it was an appeal.

Bowie nodded.

"In confidence, I'll say that I also have in mind securing horses and mules in sufficient quantity to mount the men and pull the ordnance in case we do have to retire from this position," Neill said.

"Withdraw? By God, sir, we'll never withdraw from the Alamo!" Travis cried. Command was already large upon his features. That very night he had thrown into a makeshift jail

31

five men for drunken fighting. Two of them had ridden into Bexar with Bowie.

The word spread fast. When Bowie went to his quarters that night, a delegation was waiting for him. "What's this we heard 'bout Colonel Neill a-leaving and turning things over to Travis?" Private Bijah Harriss asked bluntly.

Though he couldn't see their faces in the dark street, Bowie knew their feelings. "That's right, boys. Travis is the new commander and we're going to stand behind him."

"Huh-uh," said Private Mitchell, Kentucky. "He done throwed some of our boys in jail tonight. Claimed they oughta been out on the prairie, watching for something. That ain't all, we just don't like him, Jim."

"Won't do a-tall," someone said. "Tomorrow we elect our own man. That's the way it's got to be, or we take ever' damn' horse and mule there is and leave."

Bowie knew there was no use to argue. "Don't do anything tonight. Those boys in jail—I'll see about that tomorrow. They likely got a better place to sleep than they've been picking anyway."

"Not Bill," Harriss said. "He's been doing real good with that little señorita in the shack by the footbridge."

Another delegation was calling even then on Neill. "Colonel, sir, we got nothing much agin you," said Private Chris Parker, "but we cain't stand for having you make Travis the boss around here."

"I've got to follow military procedure!" Neill protested.

"Military procedure your ass," said another private. "We-uns is going to have an election tomorrow, and you'd best order it or we'll just up and shoot you slightly daid."

Colonel Neill saw that they weren't just funning.

Jim Bowie went to find Travis, in the house of Josefina Lopez, where Bowie was sure he would be. "Go tell your shame to your parents," he said in quick Spanish, when he walked in soundlessly on a tender scene.

"Goddamn it!" Travis cried, leaping up. "You've no right to come in on me like that!"

Josefina fled in confusion.

Bluntly, Bowie told Travis what the men of the army were thinking.

"They can't defy authority like that!" Travis said angrily.

"They can, they will. Most of them, as you damn well

32

know, are not even from Texas. They'll elect their own commander and that will be it."

"And I suppose that will be you, Mr. Bowie?"

"Yes."

"How much campaigning has gone into this little affair, may I ask?"

"Not a bit. Now look, Travis, I know what's going to happen. I want to make the best of it. You can't handle the kind of men prowling out there in the dark. I can, up to a certain point." Bowie listened to a rustling near one of the doorways at the back of the house. Well, it didn't matter, the Mexicans knew everything that was going on anyway.

Travis' voice was controlled but the anger was like a steel wire running through it. "So you too are defying authority and army discipline, Mr. Bowie?"

"Don't talk of authority and discipline to me! The so-called independent State of Texas right now is no more than hot air being blown by politicians. The only authority and discipline we'll have at Bexar is what we create ourselves, and that's what I'm trying to make you understand.

"Let the volunteers have their election. You can't stop it anyway. If they elect me I can be called commander of volunteers and you can be commander of the regulars, with neither title meaning a damn thing, except that we'll do what's necessary, the two of us working together."

Travis' shirt made a pale splash in the dark room. "No. I've been given the command."

"Listen to me, Buck—".

"No!"

Bowie grunted in disgust. He went to the cantina and told Private Harriss, "Kick in that jail and let those men out."

Harriss whacked Mitchell on the back. They let out a whoop, gathered up some companions and were on their way.

At midnight Travis came to the cantina. He saw a volunteer resting from his evening's labor on a bench outside the place and ordered him to go in and tell Bowie that Colonel Travis wanted to see him at once.

The man put a bleary eye on Travis. "Go get him yourself, soldier boy. He's right there at one of them tables."

Travis strode inside. White-faced, he went to Bowie's table in a far corner of the room. Bowie glanced at him and said, "Sit down, Buck."

33

"I understand that you gave the order to release those prisoners, Bowie."

"No order. I just told some of the boys to turn them loose. You had some of my volunteers in that goat pen, Travis."

Stiff with rage Travis said slowly, "I'm considering taking all loyal men out of Bexar and establishing a new base at Concepcion!"

"Loyal men," Bowie mused. "Loyal to who, Smith, Sam Houston, the council, God Almighty—or you?" He drank from a murky glass and made a face. "That tastes like horse piss, I'll swear." With one huge hand covering the glass, he looked up at Travis. "Take all the men who'll go with you. When are you starting?"

"Goddam you, Bowie!" Travis said in a low, tight voice. He half turned to walk out, but the knowledge that he was beaten overcame his fierce pride. He hesitated a moment longer and then he sat down.

Still angry, he said, "I have one aim, Colonel Bowie—liberty for Texas."

"I guess we're together on that." So I'm a colonel again, Bowie thought.

Travis was already forming the letter he would write to explain the compromise he had been forced to make.

When he got to it the next day, it was much simpler than most of his dispatches.

COMMANDANCY OF BEXAR
February 14, 1836
His Excellency H. Smith, Governor of Texas.
Sir . . . By an understanding of today, Col. James Bowie has the command of the volunteers of the garrison, and Col. W. B. Travis of the regulars and volunteer cavalry. All general orders and correspondence will henceforth be signed by both until Col. Neill's return.

W. Barrett Travis, Comd. of Cavalry
James Bowie, Comd. of Volunteers

NOISY AND determined, the garrison held the election and by a substantial majority named Jim Bowie as commander, little knowing that Bowie and Travis had already come to an agreement. Having asserted their rights as free men and undisciplined volunteers, the garrison resumed their formations in the cantina and other interesting places.

Taking Deaf Smith, the scout, with him, Colonel Neill went home to see his family.

At headquarters in the Avilla house that afternoon, Bowie and Travis went over the list of repairs the Alamo needed. Major G. B. Jameson, the garrison engineer, feverish with a cold, outlined the work completed so far.

"It bulks very lightly against what we have to do," he said. "We have fourteen serviceable cannon. We need five more earth platforms to place them on. We need firing ramps. The platform around the inside of the church has to be repaired, so men can fire from there. We need a well because the present ditch can be cut off easily.

"There should be, by all means, some sort of outer works, with trenches leading back to the walls of the plaza. We need—"

"We can't accomplish all your recommendations in a day." Travis leaned back in his chair. Command was a great thing, but the bothersome details of it were quite another.

"I'm getting some of it done," Major Jameson said, "by using officers. They're the only ones who want to work."

Travis flared up. "I'll issue an order to have shirkers confined!"

"You tried that," Bowie said. "Let me see what I can do, though I don't promise much."

Travis cocked his head as an uproar broke out somewhere near the main plaza. "What are they doing now? Murdering each other?"

"Wait a minute," Bowie said. He went to the door and listened. "That's what I thought. They're yelling Davy Crockett's name down there."

35

Major Jameson jumped up. "Davy Crockett! You mean Crockett is here?"

Both he and Travis started to rush out like excited boys, and then Travis remembered military dignity. "Hold it, Major! Go down there and give Colonel Crockett my compliments and tell him I request his presence at headquarters."

Bowie looked at the floor and smiled.

Half the garrison followed Crockett to headquarters, yelling and laughing and demanding stories from him. Like a giant he came striding along, a ruddy-faced man about six feet in height, with a wide grin and the disarming expression of a country bumpkin.

In spite of wanting to stand on dignity, Travis found himself at the window, gawking like the men who crowded around Crockett. "Tell us about them coons that used to yell, 'I give up!' when they seen you raisin' your rifle gun, Davy," one of the frontiersmen begged.

Grinning, Crockett stopped on the step and looked at the crowd. They were ready to laugh before he started. Good God, Travis thought, that's really Davy Crockett? That man out there in moccasins and buckskins and coonskin cap? He knew that such attire was popularly attributed to Crockett, but that he actually wore it was something of a shock.

He'd been a Congressman. He was a national figure. His feud with Andrew Jackson, his old mentor, was an outstanding subject throughout the United States. That he would now stand before a mob of grinning rabble and actually play up to them was more than Travis could grasp.

"You boys have got it wrong," Crockett said, his face suddenly sober. "Them stories you been hearing is all wrong."

Travis was relieved. Crockett was going to give them the straight of things, to disabuse some of the backwoods folk tales about him.

"Them coons never said that a-tall. First place, I never raised my rifle gun. I just sort of tunked the pan with my finger." Crockett held his famous rifle, Betsy, up for all to see and snapped his forefinger against the pan.

"That's all. Then them coons yelled. 'Don't shoot, Davy, I'm a-coming down!'"

The volunteers roared. Travis licked his lips and glanced at Jameson and Bowie to see how they were reacting. Bowie was grinning, and the Major looked as tickled as a boy who had just encountered his idol.

36

"Tell us another one, Davy!" the volunteers yelled.

"I got to see this here general fellow inside first, boys, and then I'll be along." Crockett turned and walked into the head-quarters. He took a long look at Jim Bowie, and then his keen gray eyes studied the knife on the Scotsman's thigh. "You're Jim Bowie, I swear."

The two men shook hands, and they stood there hard-gripped for a long moment, sizing each other up with some interchange of understanding that eluded Travis, leaving him an outsider in the room.

He cleared his throat and stepped forward to introduce him-self, and then Major Jameson.

"The Army of Texas welcomes you, Colonel Crockett. You've arrived at a critical time, I must say, when the forces of oppression and tyranny are massing against—" Some sly amusement in Crockett's eyes stopped Travis in mid-flight. "Uh —Colonel Crockett, will you join us in a drink?"

"That makes sense," Crockett said, and while his inflection didn't suggest that what Travis had been saying before did not make sense, still the hint of it hung in the air.

"Travis raised his glass. "To Texas and free men every-where!"

They drank to that. "Sit down, gentlemen," Travis said.

Bowie looked at Crockett's rifle and then glanced at the owner with a question in the look. Without a word, Crockett passed it around the table to him. Major Jameson scrooched his chair up close so that he too could get a close look at the famous piece.

"I assume of course that General Houston or Governor Smith sent you, Colonel Crockett?" Travis asked.

"Nope. To tell you the mortal truth, I just wandered in by myself to hit a lick, me and some of the boys."

"How many?"

"Twelve, last count, all Tennesseans."

"You—just wandered in?"

"Do you find that so startling, Colonel Travis? One thing that's said about me is quite true. Last fall before the elec-tions I said that if my constituents let Andy Jackson beat me, they could go to hell and I would go to Texas. Here I am."

It was then that Travis, who had just about come to the conclusion that he was talking to a clever buffoon, felt the weight and strength of Crockett's character. He would never fully understand the man.

He glanced at Bowie, who was absorbed in the examination of Betsy, with Major Jameson's nose so close to the lock that he might have lost the tip of it if the rifle had been cocked and snapped. Goddamn that Bowie, Travis thought.

Jim Bowie, during the moment of appraisal while shaking hands with Crockett, probably knew everything he needed to know about the man. There was a strain of something wild and simple and primitive in both of them that let them see each other without the necessity of ripping through a civilized veneer.

They'd made their marks in the West, while Travis knew that he was still a rebel without fame. Then and there his decision to gain glory from the Alamo was reinforced beyond possiblity of change.

"Colonel Crockett," he said, "I want to offer you the official status of Lieutenant-Colonel in the Army of Texas, with the responsibility of—"

"I came to fight," Crockett said, "and I thank you for your confidence in my abilities, but I prefer to be just one of the boys, if you don't mind. Besides, the Tennesseans are sort of looking to me to lead them."

"We'll assign them a leader."

Crockett grinned. "You know the only way to lead Tennesseans, Colonel? You find out where they're going and you get in front of them."

"Very well," Travis said doubtfully, and he knew that he would never know when Davy Crockett was spoofing or being dead serious. He looked at Bowie, who hadn't been one bit of help, and Jameson—the Major was staring at Crockett as if he was seeing a figure from Olympus.

"She's a fair piece, Crockett," Bowie said, handing Betsy back to the owner. "Outside of that crooked barrel, that is."

Crockett grinned. He glanced at Bowie's knife, and Bowie slipped it from the scabbard and put it before him.

Outside, the volunteers were still hanging around, calling for Crockett to come out and talk to them. And inside, the two men whom Travis secretly admitted were the natural leaders of the rabble army were comparing armament. It was just a bit confusing to Buck Travis.

When Crockett could no longer ignore the clamor of the men, he went outside and held up his hand. The quick silence that the simple gesture invoked brought a leap of jealousy in Travis.

38

"You going to be our gineral, Davy?"

"Me and Colonel Travis had ourselves a considerable of a pow-wow, and we both agreed the best thing for me was a sort of high private rank, on account of there's an awful shortage of uniforms just now."

The volunteers howled with laughter. Colonel Travis shook his head in wonder. A moment later, Crockett, Bowie and the whole mess of volunteers went trooping toward the cantina, laughing and whooping as if there wasn't a war within a million miles.

Major Jameson looked wistfully after the departing group. "Well," he sighed, "I guess I'd better get back to the Alamo to see about throwing up another platform for the cannon."

"How many men are actually working?"

Major Jameson smiled. "Six officers, one sergeant and two privates."

"I'll get you some more help, Major." Travis thought of what Crockett had said about getting in front of men to lead them. He was learning about volunteers and four-months regulars. They would gall him to the end because of their complete resistance to any semblance of military order, but they were all the force he had, and, since he was dedicated to holding the Alamo, he would do to the best of his ability that which had to be done.

Travis faced the hard truth of the matter: his background as a lawyer in the South hadn't given him an understanding of the stubborn minds and ways of frontiersmen in dirty buckskin, and his uniform and military title were not enough to bridge the gap.

But Crockett and Bowie knew the men.

If he had to be a demagogue to get something from the army, by God, he'd be one! With this entirely new approach to the problem of getting men to work on needed defenses, Travis sauntered down the street to mix with the volunteers, to appeal to Crockett and Bowie on a casual level, rather than from the throne of high command.

Travis' strategy, though he deplored the necessity of stooping to it, did result in more men reporting to Major Jameson, but still the work of patching up the Alamo was agonizingly slow.

From the south, one rumor after another came of gigantic preparations being made by the Mexican army, until both

39

officers and enlisted men profanely declared that everything they were hearing was a damn' lie.

"If I had Deaf Smith I'd send him down there," Travis told Bowie one day. "You can't believe what these Mexicans tell you."

"They know, Colonel. Believe me, they know."

CHAPTER 6

THERE WAS a coldness now and the sun was thin. The *antiguo*, Veedor Bustamente, sat on his bench with a blanket around the high bones of his old shoulders. He saw much and he heard much. He had seen the one called Crockett, and of him Veedor knew before, for who did not know of this one who could shoot birds from the air with a long rifle that bore the name of a woman?

Strange were the ways of these *tejanos*, for Crockett was a Texan as far as Veedor was concerned, no matter if it was said that he had come from far up the Mississippi. To call by a woman's name a weapon, that indeed was strange.

Other matters interested Veedor also. He called to Bernal when the boy ran from the cantina to fill a leather bucket with water, but Bernal did not come over to him until he had returned with the water.

"Where has gone Blaz Herrera, the nephew of Juan Seguin?" Veedor asked.

Bernal shifted the bucket to his left hand. "He rides to the south."

"On Juan Seguin's best horse."

"Yes," Bernal shifted the bucket again. "It is a good horse."

"I have eyes!" Veedor said testily. "I have seen horses that were horses." He scowled at Bernal. "Put the bucket upon the ground if it is so heavy."

Bernal shifted the bucket again. "Gonzalo waits for—"

"Let him wait forever. Tell me, the North American commandante sends no one to the south?"

"They will not go. They say their horses are too poor. The scouts say that." Bernal grinned. "But they go to the east on the San Antonio with messages."

Veedor grunted. "The commandante is a great fool. He

40

should know what is happening everywhere around him. Let me tell you how we did in my time. We—"

Gonzalo pushed his stomach into the doorway and shouted angrily at Bernal. "Half the morning this worthless son of mine spends listening to the lies of the old one! I cry for water. In the name of God, I need water for my cantina, and—"

"Give the pig his water," Veedor said.

Gonzalo was offended. "That is no way to talk to the one who gives his grandfather food and a warm place to sleep."

Veedor spat on the ground. He told his grandson what to do with his food and his warm place. Sometimes I think it is my anger against him that helps keep me alive, Veedor told himself; that and a desire to know the details of what goes on daily in this miserable pueblo where I must die in bed before long.

He saw Juan Seguin riding out to a little hill to stay there for a time and look to the south for his nephew. Juan thought with the North Americans, as did others in Bexar who spoke of liberty and freedom and justice.

They were fools. They would help make a country for North Americans who would then eat them up, just as the Spanish had tried to eat up the Mexicans, and as the Mexicans were now trying to eat up each other.

Liberty was in the grass, the wind, the long riding on a good horse in places where no one gave orders. That was liberty, not the noisy talk of men.

When they were very old, Juan Seguin and the others would know such things—if they lived to be very old.

That afternoon the nephew of Juan Seguin rode into Bexar on a mount that was much scratched by granjeno thorns. He reported to his uncle, who listened with care, and then Seguin went straight to Colonel Travis who was directing men in the placement of an eighteen-pounder on a dirt ramp at the southwest corner of the plaza of the Alamo.

It was brutal work. Men were tugging on ropes, some were pushing—and there were too few of them. Some of Bowie's volunteers were there, while Bowie himself was using a crowbar between the spokes of a wheel.

Travis stood at the base of the ramp, giving orders.

"I have news, Colonel Travis," Captain Seguin said.

Travis glanced at him. "All right, all right," he answered

41

curtly, turning back to the earthen platform. "One more heave there, men. All together now, heave!"

Tugging on a wheel, Private Sam Burns grunted, "That fellow has been around too many boats."

Even as extended as they were by the heavy strain, his companions gave grunting laughs. This momentary diversion helped. They rolled the cannon in place and fell against it, panting and heaving.

"Good work!" Colonel Travis shouted. He turned to Seguin. "Now, what was it, Captain?"

"I have news. My nephew has been to the Rio Grande. He has seen with his own eyes thousands of Santa Anna's men crossing with cannons."

"Where was this?"

"Near Laredo."

"Who sent him?"

"I did, Colonel."

"Why wasn't I informed that he was going?"

Captain Seguin shrugged. "I have told you now."

"Yes," Travis said. "Very well. I have another report of Santa Anna's movements."

"But it is so! My own nephew, who is to be trusted—"

"That's all, Captain Seguin."

Without saluting, Seguin walked back to his horse and rode away. Bowie walked down the ramp. His face was flushed. He felt the back of his neck and shook his head, as if to clear it. The two commanders started toward the church to see how the placing of a cannon in the apse of the structure was coming along.

Crockett and some of the Tennesseans were making an entrenchment across the weak spot that had bothered Bowie, from the corner of the church to the southern end of the low east wall of the plaza. They had appropriated two *carretas* and were using them to haul cottonwoods from the river to make a palisaded, earth-filled wall.

"I notice you ain't much for working, Davy," said Dr. Thompson, winking at his companions. "Too long in Congress?"

"I used to be a ring-tailed bearcat for grubbing between stumps and throwing dirt," Crockett drawled. "I was closer to the ground in them days. That was before I got stretched."

The whole crew quit working and leaned on their shovels. "How was that, Davy?"

"Happened when I was flatboating a load of staves down

42

the old Mississip. The boat started sinking and me stuck in this little old cabin with the door jammed and a window you couldn't throw a cat through. Well, sir, I got my head through the window and there I stuck, with the boat a-going down.

"Four, five fellows got ahold of me and started pulling. Four or five bull 'gators got ahold of the fellows and the biggest 'gator yelled, 'Heave, boys!' "

The Tennesseans looked at Travis and began to roar.

"That ain't the whole of it," Crockett said. "They pulled me through the window. I was only five feet tall when I went in that cabin, but I was six-four when they got me out. I shrunk a mite since, I'll allow."

It didn't take much to make them laugh, Travis thought sourly as he walked into the church. He looked at the cannon platforms in the apse. They were barely high enough to bear through the holes knocked in the top of the walls.

"What good will any of them cannons be, if the Mexicans get close to the wall?" Bowie asked. He looked at the wobbly platform that ran part way around the roofless part of the church. Repaired, it would be ideal for riflemen.

"It's my thought not to let them close to the walls," Travis said.

They went into the sacristy, where the Mexican army had left a great amount of defective powder. "I think I'll use the lower floor of the long barracks for an armory and magazine," Travis announced, turning back into the greater light of the auditorium.

He frowned at the debris that had fallen when the roof and towers had crumbled long before. "This has got to be cleaned up."

Bowie took a deep breath. It felt like he had strained something heaving on the eighteen-pounder. "I suppose so."

"By the way, Seguin was trying to tell me something about Santa Anna crossing the Rio Grande at Laredo recently."

"When?"

"I didn't ask." Travis shook his head. "Just another of those confounded rumors, probably. Damn, I wish we had this floor cleaned up."

"Juan Seguin is a reliable man, Colonel Travis."

"I don't doubt it, but he didn't see Santa Anna. I'm sick of listening to stories from every scared Mexican who sees a rabbit behind a bush."

They walked out the arched front door. The Tennesseans,

including Crockett, had quit work and were wandering up the plaza on some business of their own.

"I expected more responsibility from those men," Travis said in a flat tone.

"They're like any others here."

"Not quite, Bowie. They're doctors, lawyers, surveyors— the kind of men you'd naturally assume would show leadership and a willingness to accept responsibility."

"Don't naturally assume anything about men, Travis. They came here of their own free will. Just remember that."

Travis flushed under the rebuke, but he did not answer.

They walked out the main gate to their horses. Major Jameson and three other officers were building a palisade lunette beyond the porte-cochere in the middle of the south wall.

As Bowie and Travis rode away, Captain Evans mused, "Did you ever see any dust on that pretty blue uniform?"

Carretas loaded with crooked cottonwood palings were coming across the level ground between the Alamo and the river, the drivers slouching along beside them, spitting tobacco juice at the hoofs of the mules.

"Hi'ya, Jim, Buck," one of the drivers said companionably to the two commanders. "How's things going, boys?"

"Just fine, John," Bowie answered.

Travis started to rein in to give the man a sharp lecture concerning military courtesy, and then he shook his head helplessly and rode on. "What's the use?" he muttered.

Directly, they encountered other carts, a string of eight or ten of them had just forded the river. The drivers were Mexicans and their families were with them, on burros, on foot, on poor horses. Cattle and goats were mingled with the caravan.

Bowie stopped to question a tall Mexican with a Spanish musket shoulder-slung. The man was uneasy. He kept watching as the other *carretas* drew away from him. "We are not only of Bexar," he said, and pointed south and west, indicating that other families from outlying areas around the town were fleeing.

"Go with God," Bowie murmured.

The man bobbed his head and shouted at his mule.

"That story that Seguin's great-aunt invented!" Travis said. "Tell these people that there won't be any soldiers here until the middle of March, at the earliest."

"You tell them," Bowie said. "Where'd you get that information?"

"I've figured it out, based on distances, and the time it's going to take General Cos to reorganize after the beating we gave him here last December."

"That's reassuring, Colonel," Bowie said.

Travis gave him a quick look to detect sarcasm. He saw none. It seemed, rather, that Bowie just didn't give a damn when the Mexican army came. He was moody and unresponsive as they went on into town. Travis saw him staring toward the south, and then he saw him heading toward the cantina.

Lt. Charles Despalier, Travis' aide, was pacing the floor at headquarters. "I sent a man to the fort to find you, Colonel Travis. I've just received what seems to be a reliable report on the movements—"

"Of Santa Anna." Travis tossed his hat on the table. "He's crossed the Rio Grande at Laredo. Captain Seguin's grandmother's cousin saw him." Travis sat down. "Push that inkstand over here."

Despalier obliged. "Well, I thought—that is, it sounded like—"

"All those rumors are cut from the same piece of prairie wind, Lieutenant. Santa Anna, or Cos, or any other Mexican general can't possibly reach here with any force before the middle of March."

"Yes, sir," Despalier said doubtfully. "But the people of the town are running away."

"They always do." Travis began to sharpen a quill. It was time to write another letter to the Governor of Texas. . . .

The exodus of frightened Mexicans continued. Old Veedor had seen them run before, in many places in Mexico, and they had never found safety. It was a bad thing that this should happen to people always.

From San Pedro, the grandson of Veedor's old friend Amador, paused to pay his respects. This young Jose de Leon, a man of fifty years, was full of disgust. "I go now far north of the Sabine, beyond the neutral ground, and there I will stay and keep my family."

"There are many *tejanos* up there, Jose."

"Perhaps I will be like one."

"That is impossible."

45

"They fight for freedom," Jose said.

Old Veedor smiled. "Their freedom, not yours. If you wish to be a *tejano*, stay here and fight with the *tejanos* against the soldiers who are coming."

"You are not wrong in saying that they are coming, Don Bustamente. By nightfall they will be on the Medina."

Veedor's gray brows came down hard into a frown. "This is truly known to you, Jose de Leon?"

Jose nodded solemnly. He looked around the town. The North Americans were doing nothing, but being very noisy about it. They were few of them too; it was not difficult to say why Jose did not care to stay and fight with them.

Most respectfully he said good-bye to Veedor Bustamente and forthwith took his family from Bexar.

Thoughtfully Veedor considered many things, an old man who seemed to be sitting on his bench staring into nothing. He saw the mestizo couriers he had seen before, and today the sly cruelness in their faces was a smile.

He knew then that indeed the soldiers were very close, as Jose de Leon had said. The Medina was only eight miles away. A good commander, and there were many in the Mexican army, would swoop in on these lazy, careless North Americans at dawn. That is, if there happened to be a good commander.

Perhaps the North Americans should be warned.

It was an idea that did not rest well within Veedor, for, aside from Jim Bowie and a few others he had known, North Americans were no great friends of his. Of course Santa Ana was an enemy of everyone, but after he was gone, there would be another like him. One did not accomplish much by cutting the throat of one dictator, when five others were waiting to leap into his place.

Between naps, Veedor pondered the problem all afternoon. Rain swept across Bexar and passed with light effect, but off to the south there was a terrible storm, dark against the long sky.

At evening Veedor made the decision. He sent Bernal for the priest, and talked to him in a small room of the sprawling house behind the cantina. Everyone thought that Veedor was dying at last. His many relatives came wailing, and even fat Gonzalo held his head and cried out.

The old man drove them all away.

Veedor explained to the priest that many innocent people

46

would be killed if the soldiers fell upon the North Americans in the town. There would be fighting from house to house, as it had been before.

"That is true," said the priest, troubled.

"But if a message comes from a friend on the Medina, warning the North Americans, then they will go away, or they will go to the Alamo."

The priest nodded. "So you wish me to write a letter?"

"See that it is given to Jim Bowie, no other. He may believe, where the others do not believe even when they hear the truth."

"Since we speak of the truth, when are you coming to mass, Don Bustamente?"

"After the battle, if there is one. You will do this, Father?"

The priest nodded.

Huddled on the warm top of the stove, Veedor slept fitfully, hearing now and then the shouts of the fandango when he woke to ease his bad knees. The North Americans were noisier than ever.

The young Mexican pressed through the crowd and gave the note to Bowie and slipped away before Bowie had a good look at him. The dance was in full swing. Even Colonel Travis had caught the spirit of things and was attempting an elegant step before Josefina Lopez.

Bowie walked over to a fire where a group of New Orleans Greys, their once natty uniforms now torn and filthy, were working on two jugs of firewater.

"You got some good news there, Colonel Bowie?"

"Just a note from a beautiful woman," Bowie said, kneeling by the fire.

Both penmanship and Spanish were excellent. On the Medina, my God! Eight miles from Bexar.

"What's she say, Colonel?"

"She says she can't come to the fandango." On laughter, Bowie walked away to confer with Colonel Travis.

"Every time I get near a woman, you show up," Travis protested. "What is it now?"

"I think we'd better talk privately about this."

"Can't it wait till morning? I'm enjoying myself."

Brown eyes in the crowd, some soft, some glittering with hard thoughts, watched the argument between the two commanders. Bowie was insistent.

47

"All right," Travis said reluctantly, and walked up the street with Bowie to hear the matter of great concern. The weight of evidence had been growing, the flight of local inhabitants, the constant disquieting reports, and now this note, certainly not the work of some wandering mestizo.

"It could have been written by some Mexican officer," Travis said.

"Why? To warn us to prepare a defense?"

"Well, maybe to scare us into making some foolish move," Travis said uncertainly.

"If the Mexican army is on the Medina," Bowie said evenly, "they know as well as we do that it's too late for us to move any farther than the Alamo. Why would they want to scare us behind the only defense we've got?"

That made such hard sense that Travis was silent.

Louder than ever, the shouting and the stomping at the dance went on. There was love-making in the shadows, quarrels around the fires, whoops of laughter as someone told a story, and an occasional shot as some volunteer fired at the sky.

"Perhaps there *is* some basis for that warning," Travis said slowly. "In the morning we'd better send scouts out and post some sentinels." He looked back toward the fun he was missing. "Maybe that's merely a scouting patrol of cavalry on the Medina."

"It could be."

They went back to the fandango, which ran on well toward morning before the town grew quiet—except for the creaking and jolting of *carretas* leaving Bexar.

The date was then February 23, 1836.

CHAPTER 7

EARLY IN THE MORNING Private David Wilson chewed parched corn and drank water from his canteen as he lounged on top of the wall of the open bell tower of San Fernando Cathedral. Dr. John Sutherland had sent him to this post, after complimenting him for being sober the night before.

Something was stirring, sure enough. After all these months of doing nothing, and getting paid exactly nothing in the bargain, the army was showing a little life. At least they were dragging their stuff into the Alamo.

Wilson killed a hairy spider with his boot. He watched Louisianans helping themselves to possessions from a deserted house on the Plaza de las Islas below. One of them hung a string of peppers around his neck.

Day and Butler came up the street with a *carreta*-load of corn they'd found somewhere. Leave it to those Missourians to scrounge up anything that was loose. Funny how they all stuck together, the people from different states.

Wilson finished his corn. He wished he had some coffee. Maybe after a while he'd climb down and find some. He killed another spider with the rounded edge of his boot, and looked critically at the mess it made. He scraped it off against the plaster. Damn boots were about worn out.

Maybe he was sitting in a nest of spiders. He got up and moved to the next column. He could see a good distance across the rolling hills to the southwest, where Sutherland had told him to watch. For a while he'd watched like the very devil and then his eyes had begun to blear, so now he looked just occasionally.

He leaned out and spat and watched the spittle fall, swinging out in its drop before it struck the plaza. A man could crack his head falling from this height.

Wilson was looking idly at the fluting of one of the columns when movement caught the corner of his eye. He sat up straight and squinted out across the hills. Men on horses! A whole string of them, by fours!

He leaped up and began to yell and gesture. "Cavalry! Mexican cavalry!" Then he rang the bell.

Dr. Sutherland was one of the first to appear in the plaza. "Where?" he shouted.

Wilson yelled and pointed.

Before long there was an excited crowd below, and men were climbing to the dusty tower. Then Colonel Travis himself came up, brushing at his coat when he reached the gallery.

By then there was nothing in sight where Wilson had seen the horsemen but brush and the gentle hills.

"Are you sure you saw something?" Travis asked.

"Would I be yelling, if I hadn't?"

Travis peered. The others looked out at the place Wilson indicated. "I don't see nothing," a Kentuckian said.

49

"They went out of sight!" Wilson said.

"Hey, Coon," the Kentuckian said to one of his companions, "there's that Lupe gal down there that you couldn't do nothing with last night."

"Whar?"

The volunteers leaned out to look. "Clear this tower!" Travis shouted. "All of you men get back to your posts!"

"Hell, bub, no need to be so gritty about it."

"Post? What's a post, Colonel?"

The volunteers began to climb down. "Now, Private, did you actually see movement of mounted men out there?" Travis asked.

"Damn' right." Wilson gathered up his gear and began to climb down. Hell with them, if they couldn't believe a man when he told them what he'd seen with his own eyes.

Down on the plaza they were arguing about whether Wilson had seen anything. Disgusted, Wilson walked off and went in search of coffee. Travis came from the tower and found himself in the midst of an argument that bid fair to go on all morning. "A feller sometimes thinks he sees something, 'specially when he strains too hard," someone said.

Dr. Sutherland cut through the forensics with a simple statement. "There's one way to settle it." He glanced at John Smith, one of the best riders among the Americans. "Let's go take a look, shall we?"

Private Wilson, though he found no coffee, did run into a congenial group of volunteers who had taken over a house abandoned fifteen minutes before by its owners, and now they were getting ready to cook breakfast.

Plucking a freshly caught chicken, Billy Wells stood in the doorway watching activity in the plaza. "By cracky, that thar Travis is making 'em hump carrying stuff to the fort. Let's jest close these here doors and make out there's nobody but Mexicans in here."

Having evaded any sort of work up to this point, the volunteers agreed that it would be a fine idea. They shut themselves in and began to cook everything edible they could find in the house.

Wells had just got the chicken into a pot when time ran out on his culinary efforts.

Suddenly the excitement in the Plaza de las Islas took on a strongly urgent tone. Munching a cold tortilla, Wilson opened the door a crack to see what was going on. He saw Dr.

Sutherland and Smith surrounded by men. Their horses were heaving, and Sutherland's mount looked like it had been rolling in mud.

". . . at least a thousand cavalry," Sutherland was saying. "About a mile and a half, I'd say." He dismounted and his knees gave way under him.

"Did you hear that?" Wilson asked.

No one answered. They had heard, sure enough, and now they were kicking through chicken feathers as they leaped to grab their possessions. That took little time, and then they raced through the house, snatching up anything that might prove handy.

Wells grabbed the pot of chicken stew. They dog-trotted toward the footbridge. Officers were shouting, "To the fort! Every man to the fort!"

The Army of Texas, ragged volunteers and regulars in scraps of uniforms, was moving into the Alamo. No one was in a great hurry and there was laughter as they went along.

Two Alabamans paused to chase chickens through a yard. They couldn't catch them, so they calmly shot one apiece and came leaping over an adobe wall with their prizes.

"Never knowed an Alabaman yet that wasn't a chicken thief!" Wells yelled.

"Whut's that sticking all over your clothes—fur?" one of the chicken shooters jeered.

Inspired by the action of the Alabamans, Wilson shot a goat that ran bleating toward the river. His companions hooted when it seemed that he had missed, and then the goat suddenly dropped dead. Wilson cut its throat and threw it across his shoulder.

When they reached the east side of the river, the plain was dotted with men going toward the fort, some of them carrying ludicrous articles.

But all of them were carrying weapons.

Lieutenant Evans was intercepting riders. "Hold up, hold up!" he shouted. "Let's take those cows with us!"

"Now there's one officer with some sense," a horseman cried, and spurred over to raise his voice with Evans, and shortly they had a group of riders who needed no more than the suggestion of what to do.

Woe to poor Diego Sandoval! The herd that he and his cousins were even then driving toward the river was mainly

51

his, and he had suffered already at the hands of the hungry North Americans.

Now he suffered to the limit, for, with the exception of two cows that went bawling with their tails high into the cottonwoods and escaped, all the others were rounded up quickly by the North Americans and driven into the palisaded pen against the northeast corner of the Alamo.

His cousins shrugged. "They have stolen everything else in Bexar, so why not the cows?"

They went to see about the two stubborn animals that had escaped. Neither belonged to Diego. Now his cousins had their worries. The Army of Mexico was close, and Santa Anna's men also had appetites for beef. "Cursed are all these revolutions!" said Juan Marcos with great feeling.

The stream of men going toward the Alamo continued. Some of them stopped to loot the *jacals* between the river and the fort, and it was then that they discovered eighty bushels of corn, which were speedily loaded onto a *carreta* and taken to the fort.

By eight o'clock that morning the main gate was closed. Stragglers came in after that, past the unfinished breastworks in front of the chapel. Among them were twenty-one Mexicans who had decided to join in cause with the North Americans.

Near the porte-cochere Colonel Travis held council with his officers. "Now, gentlemen, let's get the things done that we should have done before." He gave orders crisply. There was a glow in his eyes. His moment of glory was on the way.

Jim Bowie's eyes held fever. He stood tall and backed Travis in command, and then Bowie took a detail to seat batteries at the north wall.

He was helping to handspike an eight-pounder up the dirt ramp when his pry pole broke. He flew backward in a six-foot drop, landing hard on his side. He didn't rise.

Private Lewis Johnson cried, "Jim's busted hisself!"

They ran the cannon back down the ramp and leaped to help Bowie.

"Leave me alone," he growled. "I hope I'm a better man than to be ruined by a little tumble like that." He got up by himself, limping and working his right hip slowly.

More men came running and Bowie waved them away. "Hand me another pry pole. Let's get these cannon placed!"

52

"There's enough of us to seat that cannon," Lewis said. "You just give orders. We'll do the work."

It was that way everywhere inside the Alamo—now. Loafers became eager workers. Major Jameson set men to digging a well, for the ditch that ran behind the church could be cut off. Crockett's Tennesseans worked on their trench and breast-works at the southeast end of the plaza with the haste of men who realized how badly it was needed.

Private Wilson, whose eyesight now came in for a good deal of praise, drew sentry duty on the west wall, and managed to get Billy Wells included in the order.

From where they stood they could see across to Bexar. The town was curiously still. The cottonwoods were moving slightly in the morning breeze, but on the hills beyond the town, where Wilson had first seen the Mexican army, there was no movement at all.

"I don't like waiting," Wilson said.

"Me neither." Wells glanced around at the frantic activity within the Alamo. "Damn, this is a big old place, and there ain't many of us, when you look from up here."

"What we've got will do." Wilson sighted his rifle at a chicken scratching near a *jacal*. He could just about knock its head off, he figured, and it was near one hundred paces away. He'd seen the soldiers first. Now it would be something big if he could kill the first one.

Colonel Travis was watching from one of the firing ramps near the southwest corner of the plaza when Lieutenant Evans brought him word of Bowie's fall.

"Is he all right?" Travis asked.

"He says so." Evans shook his head. "He doesn't look very good to me, Colonel."

"He'll be all right. He's got the constitution of a horse." Travis looked at the crew around the eighteen-pounder at the southwest corner of the plaza. There was the heaviest piece within the Alamo. He wished there were ten more like it. "Tell Dr. Sutherland I want to see him."

"He can't walk too well, Colonel. His legs are sort of bunged up from that spill when his horse rolled on him coming down that muddy hill from—"

"All right, I'll go see him. Where is he?"

"In one of those barracks, I think." Evans pointed to the buildings along the south wall.

Travis found Dr. Sutherland in one of the gloomy rooms,

53

sitting on a stool and massaging his knees. "I can still ride, if you're thinking otherwise," Sutherland said.

"Good! I want you and Smith to go to Gonzales and Goliad right away. Tell them our position here, and get all the help you can."

Sutherland nodded. "I would suggest that we wait a while until we know more about what we're facing. If there's only the cavalry that Smith and I saw, we're in no great danger."

"Every minute counts!"

"Sure." Sutherland rose to test his legs. Limping, he walked slowly across the room. "But wouldn't my appeal for help have more weight if I could honestly say that the fort was under attack when I left it?"

"The longer we wait, the greater the chance the cavalry will cut you off from going anywhere."

Sutherland hobbled back to the stool. "I think Smith and I are willing to take that chance."

Travis considered fast. Four days before he had sent Colonel John Bonham with an appeal for help, which even now might be on the way. The men of Texas were not going to stand idle when they knew the Alamo was actually under attack, even, say, if they had not rallied to Bonham's message.

"Very well, Dr. Sutherland, we'll wait a little longer to appraise the forces arrayed against us." Travis stode out to find Bowie and see for himself what shape he was in.

The Georgian was directing the emplacement of eight-pounders at the north end of the plaza. His eyes were red and his skin was flushed, and, as Evans had suggested, he appeared to have been badly jolted by his fall.

"You're feeling all right, Colonel?" Travis asked.

"Goddamn that colonel language!" Bowie flared. "Of course I'm all right. What did you expect, to see me dead from a trifling fall?"

In the chapel, Major Jameson jumped back as broken boards came down from the wooden firing platform above. He had sent Privates Ballentine and Holloway up there as sentinels and now they were clinging to posts like coons and trying to drag themselves away from the gaps where the platform had given way under them.

They made it, and Holloway called down, "This ain't much of a roost up here, by God! If a man fires his rifle the noise is likely to bring the whole works down."

"Hang on anyway and keep a sharp eye," Jameson yelled,

and went to find Travis. The work that should have been done! He was especially worried by the shacks outside the walls. They gave cover for snipers, and for work parties to come by night and dig gun emplacements and creeping trenches.

Veedor Bustamente watched them come in, lancer pennons whipping as the first troop swept by, a slender, straight-backed officer leading. Sun whipped brown faces grim above the tight chin straps of their hats. Breastplates shining. Horses mud-caked to the pasterns, mud-splattered to the withers.

A band played. The next troop went by under the Green and White and Red of Mexico. Veedor's heart quickened, though he tried to growl within himself and say that he was a fool to feel a stirring over any symbol that cried of glory and gave only the empty promises of tyrants.

Down came the gray patches of his brows when he saw riding as a sergeant of lancers Panfilio Olid, heavier now in the face, but with the same clumsy way of riding. As God was witness, Veedor Bustamente had labored hard to teach that beardless one the proper way to fit his legs around his horse and nothing had come of it, but here was Olid now, a sergeant of lancers, and he was riding no better than he had ridden those many years before.

Sergeant Olid looked toward the cantina.

That was another thing, Veedor thought. Oh, yes, my little one, were not cantinas forever in your heart? You have not changed your ways.

Old remembrance tried to speak to Sergeant Olid when he saw Veedor. His mind saw and tried to make him understand, but still he did not know. Many old men sat in the sun of Mexico, and it had been so long ago.

It came to Veedor without thought. He raised his withered right hand and put one finger against his temple, as a man holding a pistol to kill himself.

Sergeant Olid's jaw dropped. Soundlessly, he cried Veedor's name, knowing well that gesture of countless times when tough old Sergeant Veedor Bustamente had groaned in agony and threatened to blow his brains out because of the stupidness of his troop, and especially of one Panfilio Olid, of Tula.

Panfilio grinned widely in recognition, and then he was gone, trotting on toward the plaza with his troop.

Later, Veedor saw the cannon. For them he had little interest. Then Gonzalo came from the doorway of the cantina,

55

where he had been standing all the time. "Did it not appear that an officer knew you, Grandfather?"

"What if it was so?"

Gonzalo washed his hands nervously before his belly. "Having been a soldier, you know their ways. If you would speak to this officer, who could then speak to his superior officer, perhaps then my cantina—"

"Would be treated like a cathedral, where the whole Army of Mexico would walk softly and do nothing bad. This is what you desire me to ask?"

Gonzalo nodded, afraid of his grandfather's reaction, but hopeful.

Veedor grunted. "Better, I will talk to my honored friend, Santa Anna himself, and order him to make his troops behave like saints in your miserable cantina." He spat.

Gonzalo sighed and rolled his head, gazing toward the sky so that heaven itself might witness his anguish because of the cruelty and unreasonableness of this *antiguo* who was his grandfather.

"Go put your water in the wine," Veedor said. "Then it will taste better."

And still they came, column after column, and Veedor saw them with shrewd and knowing eyes. These were well-trained tough ones.

CHAPTER 8

GRIM, WIND-BURNED men watched them come from the walls of the Alamo, Travis standing on a firing ramp near the eighteen-pounder. It was the middle of the afternoon before the cavalry quit pouring into Bexar.

A flag was raised on the steeple of San Fernando Cathedral. When a breeze caught it, its blood redness lay flat against the brown hills. On the Alamo, the American rebel banner was flying, the flag of Mexico, it was, except that it had no eagle in the white, but the black numerals 1832, to denote the year when liberal concessions had been granted the colonies of Coahuila-Texas by the Mexican government.

The concessions later cancelled in anger and revenge.

56

"What's that red flag mean?" Holloway asked Ballentine. They were sitting on the chapel wall looking eastward.

"I don't know. It ain't the Flag of Mexico, I can tell you that."

"I knew that myself." Ballentine called his question down to the men working on the barricade below.

"It means free drinks for everybody," a wag said.

After the laughter, someone gave the correct answer.

"That means no quarter!"

"We ought to have one ourselves to wave back at them bastards," Holloway said.

Travis called over to the cannoneers around the eighteen-pounder: "Lay your sights on that red flag! I'll give you the word when I want you to fire."

"She'll never reach," Cannoneer Bob Hutchinson said to his crew, but he followed the order and elevated the piece.

Standing by with a swab in his hand, Private Linn squinted at activity across the river. "I think they're getting a battery in place over there."

In his British accent Private Richard Dimkin said, "Undoubtedly no more than a little salute gun to call us to breakfast every morning."

Travis frowned when he heard the cannoneers laughing.

At their post in the middle of the west wall, Weils and Wilson lay on the roof of a barracks behind bags of earth they had carried up. They had an excellent view of the trees along the river and the collection of huts on the east side of the San Antonio.

Occasionally they had a clear glimpse of soldiers in the town, but, although Wilson was on edge to get in the first killing shot, he knew his rifle wouldn't carry with accuracy into the town. He waited.

He was rewarded. He saw movement on the footbridge. Wilson cocked his piece, sighted down the barrel and took a deep breath.

And then he saw the white flag in the hands of a Mexican officer when he came to the middle of the bridge. Wilson let his breath out and cursed. "Just when I thought I had me something."

The officer came on farther. The clear call of a bugle rolled out across the plain. A Mexican who had stayed almost too late in one of the *jacals* a hundred yards away came out and ran toward the river, misreading the bugle call.

57

"That's the parley call," Wells said. "We learned that last winter when we took Bexar."

"What's there to talk about?"

Near the base of the eighteen-pounder platform, Colonel Travis was asking the same question of Bowie. "What can they ask—besides demanding our surrender?"

"We ought to go talk, at least. It's that much more time, Travis."

"No! I refuse to parley. We're here for one purpose, to fight!"

Bowie obviously was seriously ill, and that helped increase his evil mood. "You do as you damn please with the fighting, after it gets started, Travis, but I'm sending a man out with a white flag."

"Are you trying to destroy the discipline of this force?" Travis asked angrily.

"No, by God, but I am gaining a little more time to work on the defenses!"

Travis turned and walked away.

The parley call sounded again.

An instant later Travis himself put the match to the touch-hole of the eighteen-pounder. It boomed out heavily. The ball was far short of the target. "Elevate!" Travis cried.

"She won't reach, Colonel," Hutchinson said.

In cold anger Bowie was writing a note. He called the cannon shot a "misunderstanding." To Major Green B. Jameson he said, "Benito, are you up to taking this out and exchanging the courtesies with their representative?"

Jameson nodded. He was on his way soon afterward.

The bugle continued to call its strident question.

Colonel Travis was still tinkering with the cannon sights, getting ready for another shot, when Linn said, "Who's that going out to parley?"

Bitterly, angrily, Travis watched Major Jameson riding toward the footbridge. Silently he cursed Jim Bowie.

At the barricade in front of the church, Crockett picked up Betsy and grinned at his Mounted Volunteers. "You cavalry folks keep digging. I got to go watch this parley pow-wow." He leaped the low wall and went striding away.

"Cavalry," said Dr. Thompson, looking at his shovel.

The Mounted Volunteers laughed.

A dozen men had crowded up near Wells and Wilson, but the two paid no attention to them, intent on watching Major

Jameson. He was carrying a white flag and his sorrel was gleaming in the sun as he trotted toward the bridge.

"If that Mexican officer ever looks like he meant harm, drill the bastard!" someone said.

A man crowded in beside Wilson, saying, "How about a piece of your firing place, bub?"

Wilson didn't look at him, but he grunted, "If you wasn't so damn lazy, you could carry your own dirt up here."

Jameson went in and out between the *jacals* and on to the footbridge. He dismounted and exchanged salutes with the Mexican officer.

"I never could understand that," someone grumbled. "You figure on killing each other in a minute or two, but you salute and say, 'Howdeedo, sir, and how's your health today?'"

"You just ain't polite, Bill, that's all."

The parley did not last long. Major Jameson rode back and delivered a message to Bowie, who received it in the plaza with men crowding around him. He scanned it quickly and passed it on to Travis.

After a few moments Travis cried, "What did I tell you? All they want is for us to place ourselves at the disposal of the supreme government. Indeed!"

The men crowding around Bowie kept asking, "What did old Santa Anna say, Colonel?"

Bowie put it simply. "Surrender immediately—or die."

"Surrender, hell!"

"Not us!"

"I'll take the dying!"

And that was the spirit of the Alamo. A moment later the eighteen-pounder fired with a boom that rocked around the plaza. Gunner Hutchinson watched the ball in flight, and shook his head. The defenders of the Alamo had stated their defiance, twice, but again the shot was not going to reach the red flag on the steeple of San Fernando church.

Hutchinson was right.

In the shed where he had hidden his five goats from the clutches of hungry North Americans, and where they were still hidden, Manuel Madero had just brought them forage, and was strolling away casually so that the Mexican soldiers would not think he had anything of importance in that shed.

Behind him he heard a *whushing* sound and then a terrible crash. "Mother of God!" he yelled, and turned to see his shed in ruins. Out of the dust and debris came his five goats, bleating in terror but unharmed.

And then grinning Mexican soldiers gathered them in. There was no way for a poor man to win, Manuel thought sadly. And he had been to mass and confession as often as any man in Bexar who owned goats.

"Why, it's Mister Davy Crockett hisself!" Private Wilson said, when he had time to look at the man who had crowded in on him.

"At your service, bub," said Crockett, looking down his rifle gun with both eyes open.

A moment later he fired. A Mexican soldier in the town, walking unhurriedly over to see what the cannon ball had done to Manuel Madero's goat shed, fell dead with a ball in the head.

"That ain't possible!" Billy Wells gasped. He had been considering taking a just-for-the-hell-of-it shot at that same Mexican himself.

"Ain't it?" said Crockett. "You go over and ask him, if you don't think so." He stood up, his face stone sober. "Shooting at such a distance is mighty hard on a rifle, though. That shot might have strained old Betsy here until she won't be worth a damn from now on."

As usual, whenever Davy Crockett said something, there was an explosion of laughter. Grinning, Crockett went back to help put the final touches on the earthworks he and his men had been assigned to defend.

Travis and Bowie both considered it the most vulnerable spot of the entire mission.

"Well, I think we can consider that we're now under attack, Dr. Sutherland," Travis was saying in one of the rooms of the south barracks. "Are you ready to go?"

Sutherland nodded. He looked at John Smith, who said, "I'm ready."

Sutherland rode out until he struck the sunken road to the east of the fort, which gave him fair cover until he reached a grove of trees. From the cover of the cottonwoods he looked back to see if there was pursuit. So far, none.

Ten minutes later, John Smith left the fort, following the same route. The two couriers joined later on the low hills several miles from the Alamo.

They heard the opening fire of the Mexican artillery and

60

stopped their horses to listen, looking quietly at each other, and then they rode again to carry out their mission.

A lookout on the chapel shouted, "Rider! Rider coming from the east!"

Travis' first thought was that Sutherland or Smith had been turned back by Mexican cavalry, but a moment later the sentinel shouted, "No one's chasing him!" And then he added, "He's got a rag on his hat."

"Bonham!" Travis said, and he was right.

When the gates opened and Colonel John Bonham brought his dun horse into the Alamo, half the garrison came rushing to see what news he had, but Travis and other officers shouted men back to their work.

Travis and the courier conferred in the command post in one of the rooms of the south barracks.

Bonham stood about six feet two, black-haired, dark-eyed. Like Travis, he was a born rebel. They had been boyhood friends in the Edgefield District of South Carolina, and later, both of them had practiced law in Alabama.

"Any trouble on the ride?" Travis asked.

Bonham shook his head, walking about the room as he worked saddle stiffness from his legs. "Colonel Fannin can't send any help from Goliad right now. He says he's got to hold the fort there, in case Santa Anna swings on east."

In the name of God and Texas! This was the vital spot, and it was already under attack, not Goliad. If the Alamo fell, then Goliad and all of Texas was wide open. Travis held his rage down. "Any movement of Mexican cavalry east of here?"

"None that I saw."

"There will be," Travis predicted. With all the troops of cavalry the Mexicans had, it wouldn't take them long to throw strong patrols across the Gonzales road. Sutherland was right, though; once it was known that the Alamo was under siege, help would be forthcoming, and if the reinforcing column had to fight its way through a screen of cavalry, Texans could do that too.

"Get some rest, John. You need it."

Travis went out to see what moves the Mexican army was making. He was not long in finding out.

Before he had crossed the plaza on his way to the big gun, explosions crashed all along the west wall of the fort. He ran up to a firing platform. Puffs of smoke showed him where the enemy artillerymen had emplaced two batteries on the west

61

side of the river, one almost due west, the other near a low building to the southwest.

He could see the lazy flight of the balls coming at the mission, and by the sounds of the explosions and the lack of damage they did against the nearly three-foot-thick west wall, he judged that they were six-pounders. He laughed.

Santa Anna would have to do much better than that if he wanted to make any headway.

Gunner Hutchinson called over, "Shall we reply, Colonel? We've got 'em spotted."

"Fire away!"

The eighteen-pounder boomed in a ranging shot. Dust bloomed at the corner of the long, low building across the river. The gunners shouted. "To hell with the building!" Hutchinson said. "We want the gun." He looked at his spongeman. "Well, Linn, is this the only shot of the war?"

Private Linn was watching where the ball had struck. "Oh!" he said, when Hutchinson's words struck home, and dipped his sponge and went to work.

Hutchinson laid the sights again. "Fire in the hole!" he yelled. The cannon bucked and roared, and then the gunners yelled in earnest when they saw a shower of dirt erupt and fall on the enemy cannon.

For an hour the big gun of the Alamo duelled with the two batteries across the river—and silenced them. A cheer went up from the men on the walls, and even Travis let go with a shout when the piece directly west fell silent.

At his sniper's post on the barracks near the old convent courtyard, behind an earth-filled cowhide, one man did not cheer. He was Louis Rose, nicknamed Moses, a well-knit, bearded little man who had fought under Napoleon Bonaparte across the map of Europe.

He knew how light the batteries were that had opened against the Alamo. Most surely the army across the river had bigger pieces that would come into play later. This fort—and that was giving the place a great benefit—was not good.

All the open ground around it. Not good. No outworks to take the brunt of rushes. Day by day, entrenchments could be extended by the attackers, creeping closer, until no man within would dare show his head above the walls.

There was a matter of food, also. And powder—Rose had looked into the magazine. Too little. He looked at the horses penned in one corner of the convent yard. No longer did he have a horse of his own, and it would be a long, dangerous walk to leave this place.

And then he saw a troop of cavalry swooping out to the east. Ah, of course! They would invest the eastern approach to the Alamo, and try to make it most difficult for men to come or to leave.

A while longer, Rose thought, I will stay to see what happens. Perhaps the new nation that the Americans talked so much about was really in the making in this wild place. If they won, and the nation became a fact, those who had fought to make it so would be rewarded, would they not?

At dusk the batteries that had fallen silent opened up once more.

"I thought we got them," Linn said.

Gunner Hutchinson spat. "Maybe we did, and maybe they just hauled back to wait. You think they got only *two* guns, do you?"

This time they saved powder by not firing the eighteen-pounder. In the dusk the sights could not be laid, and the pieces across the river were more nuisance than anything else, even when they fired solid rounds, which only bumped the west wall and fell to the ground.

After dark Travis sent outposts east and north of the Alamo to guard against surprise attack by night, and to determine if the *jacals*, which should have been torn down during the long and pleasant days of waiting, were invested by Mexican forces.

Small fires sprang up within the walls. Volunteers and regulars, having had a small whiff of powdersmoke together, mingled freely with each other, roasting meat on ramrods, insulting each other friendly-like.

"I heard big talk about a fearful huge Texas army," Private William Marshall said, "but I ain't seen nothing but ragged-assed loafers sence I been here. And what army they is—I ain't found a fellow yet that was born in Texas. You fellows tell me the downright truth now—is they one man here that was really born in Texas?"

No man could answer yes until Juan Abamillo said, "We are born in Texas." He pointed to his companions, Antonio Fuentes, Domingo Losoyo, Gregorio Esparza, whose wife and children were in the Alamo, and a dozen more Mexicans, mainly of Juan Seguin's company.

Marshall strode around the fire to clap Abamillo on the shoulder. "I knew it! They ain't a native-born Texan in the

63

whole damn kit and caboodle except these fellows right here!"

Slicing meat with his Arkansas toothpick, James Rose said, "Who besides them has had time to be born here? I'm from Nacogdoches and that makes me a Texan, no matter where I was born."

"We're going to have a vote," Marshall announced, "and change the name of this here bunch to the Army of Tennessee, helped some by Nacogdoches Volunteers. All in favor—"

"You'll crap and fall back in it too!" a Texan yelled.

They whooped and jeered, while six-pound batteries kept popping away at the walls. For all the men of the Alamo cared, those guns might have been throwing balls of cotton.

Wilson and Wells had learned one thing about those popguns: you didn't lean out to see where the shell was going to hit when you saw it coming. They'd made a bet about that. Wells said a particular shot wasn't going to reach the wall, and Wilson said it was.

They both leaned out to see where it struck, and when it exploded Wells got his right ear ripped by a whizzing rock fragment and Wilson took a cut across the forehead.

They guessed they were just about the first wounded in the Alamo, and so proud of the fact they hadn't bothered to wash the blood away.

Lieutenant Dickerson came by. "Boys, we're going to have to watch our fires. We haven't got much wood in here."

"Fair enough, Lieutenant."

When Dickerson passed on to the next fire with his warning, a man said, "His wife and kid are both in here. I wouldn't much like that for my family."

For a few moments those who had children somewhere were silent, thinking about them.

Six men from the Brazos who had straggled into Bexar just a few days before, were giving a good deal of thought to their families on far-scattered ranches. They gathered on the wall above the cattle pen to discuss the situation.

They took an informal vote. An hour later, leading their horses, they told the sentry on the main gate that they were going out on a night scout. He didn't question them, but opened one gate wide enough for them to slip into the darkness—and out of history.

They were not the only ones who balanced wisdom against

heroism. About half of the twenty-one Mexican civilians who had cast their lot with the North Americans went over the east wall that night, across the Acequia de Villita that ran just behind the chapel, then southwest on a wide swing that brought them back to the outskirts of Bexar where they slipped in unnoticed.

Jim Bowie by then was lying on a cot in a room in the south barracks that was also a granary. "You want more water, Mistuh Jim?" Ham, the Negro boy, asked, his eyes rolling white in the candlelight.

Bowie sat up to drink, shaking his head against the hated feeling of weakness in him. It wasn't just the fall he'd taken. He realized that now. At least two days before that he'd felt a touch of fever coming on.

He started to rise when Travis came to the doorway, and then he sank back.

"How are you feeling?" Travis asked.

"Not worth a damn."

"I'll send Dr. Pollard over—"

"Never mind! I've had fever before. Purge or bleed. To hell with that."

Travis hesitated. "Suppose you don't feel well enough to exercise your share of command in—"

"Don't worry!" Bowie lay back, his eyes open and staring at the ceiling. "I'll back you as commander of this rat hole."

Travis left with the certain knowledge that Jim Bowie was too sick to be a force in affairs from then on. In that light he could forgive Bowie all their past differences.

He looked toward dark forms sleeping on their arms at the breastworks. Now that danger was really at hand, those Tennesseans were a solid unit of dependability. He had no doubt that they would deal out all the misery Santa Anna cared to receive if he hit their position.

He went on up the plaza and into the southern room of the long barracks along the east wall. Both Dr. Mitchasson and Dr. Pollard were there, gravely discussing how little they had in the way of medical supplies for the long, gloomy room that was the hospital.

They already had patients, those who had fallen ill during the long stay in Bexar and those still not recovered from wounds received during the taking of the town in December.

Travis started to explain about Bowie. Dr. Pollard cut him

65

short. "He has pneumonia, Colonel, and there's not much we can do for him."

Mitchasson took a candle from a table and lit a short cigar. The light shone richly on his brown spade beard as he studied Travis. "He'll get well, or he won't, depending on circumstances."

"Did you examine him?" Travis asked.

"Yes. Under the guise of looking for broken bones after his fall," Pollard said.

"Do everything you can for him," the commander said, and went out.

From a firing ramp Travis looked across the night at the enemy. Here and there a fire winked to the east and south where units of the Mexican army were encamped. Between rounds of the light batteries, fired to harass the sleep of the men in the Alamo, he heard soft music in the town.

He was in sole command now. He felt strong and sure. Santa Anna would never crack the Alamo before reinforcements came from Goliad and elsewhere. And after that . . . why, it was not beyond hope that Travis could lead the Army of Texas in their own attack, as he had done when he took Anahuac in '31, and Nacogdoches in '32.

There was a feeling of glory to come in the cool night air. Buck Travis breathed deep of it.

In the chapel, a handful of women had quieted the children and got them to sleep at last, Mrs. Dickerson's baby and little ones of the families of Mexicans still in the mission. Mrs. Horace Alsbury was there, the adopted daughter of Veramendi, Jim Bowie's dead father-in-law.

Stars looked through the open part of the roof. Boards creaked up there along the wall as sentries moved with extreme care on the flimsy firing platform. Earth piled where the altar had been made a platform for three cannon, strange and deadly intruders in a church.

Tired and worried, the women lay down. They found no glory in the Alamo.

CHAPTER 9

COMMANDANCY OF THE ALAMO, BEXAR
February 24th, 1836
To the People of Texas and All Americans in the World—
Fellow Citizens and Compatriots: I am besieged with a thousand or more of the Mexicans under Santa Anna. I have sustained a continual bombardment and cannonade for 24 hours and have not lost a man. The enemy has demanded a surrender at discretion, otherwise, the garrison are to be put to the sword, if the fort is taken. I have answered the demand with a cannon shot and our flag still waves proudly from the wall. *I shall never surrender or retreat.* Then I call upon you in the Name of Liberty, of Patriotism, and everything dear to the American Character to come to our aid with all dispatch. The enemy is receiving reinforcements daily and will no doubt increase to three or four thousand in four or five days. If this call is neglected I am determined to sustain myself as long as possible and die like a soldier who never forgets what is due his own Honor or that of his country.
VICTORY OR DEATH!

William Barrett Travis
Lt. Col. Comd't

Travis signed his name with a strong hand. It was the third draft of the appeal he had made in his headquarters room in the south barracks. First, he had addressed it to the people of Texas only, and then he had enlarged it to appeal to Americans everywhere. Native honesty told him that there was more than he needed in the salutation, but he justified it on the basis of emergency.

His background of law practice had taught him that men were moved more by emotion than by reason.

Now, a messenger to carry it.

Lieutenant Dickerson came in. He had been up most of the night, inspecting defenses, cautioning sentinels against dozing. He slumped into a chair with a sigh and stretched his legs out.

"How is Mrs. Dickerson taking things?" Travis asked.

67

"Well enough." Dickerson added, "As well as any woman could under the circumstances."

Travis hesitated. "We could request a parley and send our non-combatants out."

Dickerson shook his head. "My wife wouldn't go. She's told me that already."

"We'll be relieved. I'm sure of it." Travis' mind flicked back to the dispatch on the table. How could the people of Texas ignore that? He started to push the message across the table to Dickerson, and then he saw that the lieutenant's head was dropping in little jerks as he fought against dozing.

"Joe!" Travis called to his Negro servant.

"Yes, Colonel Travis." Joe came to the doorway, a very black, good-looking, intelligent man of about twenty-three, whom Travis had brought with him from Alabama five years before.

"Bring the lieutenant some coffee, Joe."

The small cooking fire was outside. Joe returned shortly with a black, steaming pot. As he poured the coffee he kept eyeing the double-barrelled cap and ball pistol that Dickerson wore. "That sure is a fine pistol, Lieutenant."

Travis allowed himself a smile. "Never mind, Joe, I'll see that you get one before too long."

As Joe turned to go outside, men moving on the log and cement roof of the building caused small particles of rock to fall in a shower on Travis' message. He snatched it up and shook it. Then he reached across the table and laid it before Dickerson. "What do you think of that?"

Dickerson had taken a sip of the scalding coffee. As he leaned forward to read, a drop of the liquid fell from his lips on the paper. He blew at it, then wiped it away with his finger.

Travis frowned.

Lieutenant Dickerson kept blinking his eyes as he read slowly. After some time, he said, "That ought to do, I'd say."

Travis was disappointed, but Dickerson was either too tired to observe that, or he didn't care. He took another sip of coffee and asked, "Are you writing a dispatch, or something for posterity?"

Travis colored, on the verge of a sharp answer, and then he thought, Posterity? Why not? When this siege was lifted and the Mexican army scattered, that message would be something for men to look to and remember. He'd send it out within the hour by the most trusted and reliable courier he could select.

The coffee was rousing Dickerson from his momentary lethargy. "I'm wondering, Colonel Travis, if it's wise to keep reducing our force here by sending couriers. We've already sent—"

"Some of them may not have got through."

"Bonham did."

"He's an exceptional man. His last message was delivered before we were actually under siege, when no one knew where the Mexican army was. Now they know, and it's up to me to keep them informed!"

Dickerson glanced down at the bottom of the paper. VICTORY OR DEATH! Oh, he guessed he'd shouted a few highflown words in his time, and even believed them; but that was before he had a wife and child, and damn' well before that wife and child were penned up in a crumbling mission.

He rose. "I'll take another tour around." At the low doorway he hesitated. "That big gun is using twelve pounds of powder per shot, Colonel Travis."

"I know. We may have to cut down on our artillery fire before the siege is over."

Lieutenant Dickerson blinked in the sunlight when he walked into the plaza. He saw his wife and some of the other women washing clothes in leather buckets near the courtyard gate in the low eastern wall.

Captain Bill Blazeby, of the New Orleans Greys, came down a ladder from the roof, jumping the last few feet. "They've swung a force across from the south and are coming in toward those huts." He ducked inside to see Travis.

Already there was a shifting of defenders along the walls. They could see, or they had the word from others who could see, where danger threatened, and now they were coming on the run toward the south end of the plaza.

"Stay at your posts!" Dickerson shouted.

A few who were shifting to the south saw the sense in that and went back to their assigned positions. Other officers were shouting at the volunteers. Discipline, Dickerson observed, had improved enormously.

He glanced at the barricade. The Tennesseans were standing firm, although some of them had leaped up on the earthworks to see what was going on. Crockett was ambling toward the south barracks. He turned toward his men and called,

69

"You boys just rest easy. Everybody will have all the shooting he wants before she's done."

Dickerson went up on the roof, and a moment later Travis joined him.

"They make a purty sight, I do declare," a Texan said, leaning on his rifle as he looked toward the river to the southwest.

Two or three hundred Mexican infantrymen had crossed the San Antonio and were working toward the *jacals,* advancing in loose formation, their uniforms making bright splashes against the drab plain. Behind them came a horse-drawn battery.

"We can't have that gun seated close to us," Travis said. "Captain—"

Close to him a rifle spat. Powdersmoke drifted along the rooftop with an acrid odor. One of the horses pulling the cannon dropped dead. "Is that what you mean, Colonel?" Crockett asked. " 'Course that ain't going to stop 'em, but it do sort of convey the idea."

Rifles began to crack all along the roof. The second horse reared and went down.

"That's too much shooting for one poor horse," Crockett observed, and his calm, amused tone did more to stop the long range firing than a dozen shouted orders.

Travis sized up the situation quickly. "Let them into range, and then, for God and Texas, pick them off!"

"Aim to," a South Carolinian drawled. "I don't know 'bout God and Texas," he murmured to a companion, "but we'll roll 'em over for somebody."

A second team of horses was coming on the gallop toward the stranded cannon.

Beside the dead horses, Lieutenant Alonzo Hernandez of the Matamoros Battalion sat his gray horse Alcazar with easy grace. How stunned and stupid looked the cannoneers, to know that bullets from guns that made so little noise could reach this far to kill the animals. He wasted but an instant on that thought.

"Cut the harness, idiots," he ordered calmly, then turned and waved for the men riding the backs of the reserve team to make haste. Of *Gachupine* father and Creole mother was Lieutenant Hernandez, a man of grace and handsome features, and to him bravery and honor were a way of life.

"Swing the cannon, *zongos!* You cannot drag it over dead

70

horses!" He turned to look at his infantry advancing on ahead. They trotted half crouched, as if to be smaller targets. That was the Indian in them.

Sweating heavily, Sergeant Archuleta heaved and grunted with his men and got the cannon turned away from the still legs of the horses. They hitched the team to it and turned to advance farther toward the huts, where Lieutenant Hernandez had orders to seat the battery.

This time there wasn't even a rearing. One horse went down. The other staggered from the weight thrown so suddenly on it by the harness, and then it too dropped without so much as a sigh or grunt.

An instant later the cannoneers heard two tiny *poofs!* carrying to them from the Alamo. Sergeant Archuleta looked at a small hole in the head of each horse, and then he stared at the wall of the fort. What kind of devils fired like that at such great distance?

In truth, Lieutenant Hernandez was somewhat startled himself, but he said calmly, "Now we have four dead horses. You will pull the cannon, Sergeant, with your men." He spun Alcazar in a turn that threw clouts of earth. He intercepted a squad of infantry and sent them to help drag the cannon.

He saw infantrymen falling as he trotted ahead. They went down suddenly, with no heroics, no clutching of the breast, no struggling or crying of God and country. They died most simply, pitching forward on their faces, then lying in still, huddled bundles on the ground.

It did not occur to him to dismount and lead his horse to make himself less of a target. He was an officer of the Mexican army, the son of a *Gachupine,* not some *mestizo* who longed to scuttle to shelter when the first bullet sang past.

The only firing that was loud was from the men ahead, who sometimes shot their muskets as they ran, without getting them fully to their shoulders. To stand and reload in the open was to die, and so they hurried on when their muskets had been fired.

Alcazar reared suddenly when the dry song of a rattlesnake sounded, and it was then that the brave gray horse that had stood the march so well was killed by a bullet speeding straight toward Lieutenant Hernandez's throat.

Only his years of horsemanship saved Hernandez from having his right leg caught under the gray as it went down.

71

He kicked free just in time and went pitching to one side, skidding on his shoulder. He rose quickly and brushed at his coat, before he drew his sword and ran forward to where the infantry were hesitating in a little swale that gave them some protection.

"On, you dogs, on!" he shouted, and began to whack the hesitant ones across the rumps with his sword. One Pablo Padilla was recharging his musket, and him Hernandez did not disturb. But he beat the others on and cursed a sergeant who was as fearful of his life as the others.

The congestion in the little hollow began to break. A sergeant came up with the next squad and stayed to see that no one cringed here when there was glory up ahead.

Hernandez looked back toward the battery. Men were pulling it, but they were falling. Others took their places, and they fell too. Sergeant Archuleta—and this was a thing to remember when reporting to Captain O'Donnojou—was kicking to their feet those who wished to lie down, and waving to the infantrymen trotting by to come and help.

Hernandez went back. He stopped some of the foot soldiers and sent them to drag the cannon. They pulled it for a distance, their number dwindling as the little balls came singing and chopped into their heads, and then the rest scattered away from the piece that drew death as a flower draws bees.

A third time Lieutenant Hernandez rallied men to pull the cannon, but they did not get far with it before the trail of blue-coated bundles grew behind them, until there were too few left to do the work.

Sergeant Archuleta waved his arms and looked helplessly at his lieutenant. Herandez waved his sword for him to follow and the two of them ran on to the little hollow, where the same Pablo Padilla, crouched, was once more recharging his *escopeta*.

On ahead were the *jacals*, where the men of the Matamoros Battalion were to tear down buildings to secure timbers for the making of a bridge across the San Antonio. Some of the infantry were already running toward them.

And then the cannons from the fort began to boom.

Whistling objects, and pieces of things that whined or shuddered, came driving through the air. They scared the foot soldiers, but Lieutenant Hernandez, who had heard cannons before, observed coolly that only two or three of the soldiers had been hit.

72

"On!" he shouted to the huddlers. He was about to go across the open ground himself, when a great suspicion about Pablo Padilla came to him. He turned and watched the man. Yes, that brave soldier was even again reloading his musket.

Smiling, Lieutenant Hernandez walked over and touched him with his sword point. "Fire. Fire at that big one there on the wall of the fort who wears the strange animal on his head."

"I cannot see him well, my lieutenant." Pablo shook his head, pleading.

Hernandez jabbed him lightly in the rump with the sword and Pablo leaped up with a yelp. "Now you can see him well, the big one who stands there shouting insults, even as he reloads his musket. Fire at him!"

"Mercy of God!" Pablo cried.

Hernandez drew the sword back. "Fire!"

Pablo took the only chance he had. He lifted his musket, closed both eyes tightly and aimed in the general direction of the fort. Inside the barrel of his *escopeta* was charge on charge. As Lieutenant Hernandez leaped back nimbly, the musket blew apart with terrible noise.

It fell from Pablo's hands. He reeled back, clutching the bloody welter of his face, bubbling in agony.

Sergeant Archuleta blinked and felt his own face, where a piece of the exploding musket had slashed his cheek. He ran his tongue into the hole and it came to the outside.

"Remeber what you have seen and learn from it," Lieutenant Hernandez advised him. "Now, forward!"

No one lagged now, or crouched to load a musket that was already loaded.

The cannons knocked down three more men, who scrabbled on the ground, kicking and groaning, but many of the men of the Matamoros Battalion reached the *jacals* and kept working in until they were no more than a hundred paces from the fort, and there, carrying out their orders, officers began to direct men in the wrecking of the buildings.

Coolly, Lieutenant Hernandez looked back, wondering if even yet he could get the cannon up here, but he saw that his superior officers had sent more horses and more men, and they were dragging the cannon back toward the river.

The cannons of the fort kept shouting, but they were doing no great harm. It was the hard spats of the riflemen on the walls that kept killing soldiers. A man moved across an open

73

space. He fell. Angel Medina stepped out to fire. The musket dropped from his hands. He was dead. Erasmo de Rado crawled upon the roof of a *jacal*, nestling down in the straw. He fired twice, and then he lay there and his musket tumbled to the ground.

When the cannons were not booming, Lieutenant Hernandez and the others could hear the loud shouting from the tall one with the hat of animal skin. Sometimes it seemed that he was almost friendly with the things he said, and now and then he sang.

When he reloaded his tall rifle, he stood up in plain view. An accurate observer, even under stress, Hernandez noted that when the tall one fired, a soldier died, and almost all of those who died by rifle fire were shot in the head or in the throat.

Soon it was more than the officers could do to keep the men working to get timber.

Lieutenant Manzanares came up beside Hernandez where he leaned against a wall, watching the fort through an angled opening between two *jacals*. Grim and angry, Manzanares said, "From this place there will not be carried back enough wood to warm the murderer's coffee." From Zacatecas he was, where many people had no love for Santa Anna.

Hernandez shook his head, cautioning against such talk where soldiers could hear. His own father was in great disfavor with Santa Anna. On the terrible march from Laredo the young officers had laughed and joked, saying that Lieutenant Hernandez was sure to have the opportunity for glorious leadership, since Santa Anna would see that he was given the most exciting and dangerous assignments.

"If it is possible to carry away the wood, we will do it," Hernandez said.

A soldier with a plank on his shoulder turned to carry it toward the river. He fell and the plank lay across his back, still a burden, though he was dead.

Manzanares spat. "The Napoleon of the West! He has said it himself."

Once more Lieutenant Hernandez cautioned against such careless talk before the men.

From the trees along the river a bugle sounded its sharp, urgent call to retreat.

"Ah!" said Manzanares. "General Castrillon, at least, has some sense in his head."

74

Before he left, Hernandez took careful aim with his pistol, allowing for the distance, aiming at the tall one with the fur of animals upon his head. He fired and the bloom of powder-smoke obscured his vision, but when it cleared the tall one was still there, laughing loudly at something. A devil from hell, Hernandez thought.

Back to the river they went, the men of the Matamoros Battalion, without wood for the bridge, without many of their comrades, with nothing but honor for trying hard and well to carry out an impossible order so close to the deadly rifle fire of the ragged men of the Alamo.

As he passed the body of Alcazar, that one of great heart and stamina, Lieutenant Hernandez shook his head sadly. By night he would come and get the saddle and bridle.

Sergeant Archuleta caught up with Pablo Padilla, staggering along blindly and calling upon saints for things they could not do for him. The sergeant took him by the arm. "Come along, my brave one. If the lesson has not killed you, the next time you will not hide in a safe place and pretend that you are killing the enemy with one shot after another."

On the walls of the Alamo, a wild, exultant jeering followed the retreating soldiers.

Lieutenant Hernandez puzzled over something strange that had troubled him since the first cannon horse fell dead. Now he recognized what it was. It was the first skirmish he had been in when no bullets sang wildly around his ears. Yes, that was it. Except one time, when the second horse of the cannon had been killed, there had been no splats of earth in front and no poorly aimed balls flying overhead.

The bullets of the North Americans had come only to kill the soldiers they were aimed at, not to scare the cooks and musicians and generals in the rear.

It was well that the North Americans did not use their cannons as they did their rifles, or the Napoleon of the West would find it most difficult to send men against the fort.

Colonel Travis was jubilant. He congratulated the men of his command—it was his command solely now, since Jim Bowie, rising from his sick bed, had called the garrison together and told them to follow Travis' orders without question.

Such a signal repulse of the Mexican forces deserved a letter. Travis went to write it.

Louis Rose, the former mercenary, had been in the fight and

he had seen the deadly accuracy of the rifle fire. Name of a name! That was something to speak of, even though it was not the first time Rose had seen American frontiersmen in action.

Of the handling of the cannons—that was another thing entirely. The gunners fired them, to be sure, but they did not know their business well. And placed as they were on piles of earth, with too little room on top, the pieces could not be used to their greatest advantage to fire in many directions.

It occurred to Rose that he could make good suggestions about improving the emplacement of the artillery, but he shrugged away the thought of doing so. His English was not good. In fact, sometimes he had been mistaken for a Mexican when he spoke, although those who had come from New Orleans knew quickly that he was French when he talked to them.

Now that it would be quiet for a time while the Mexican commander decided what next to attempt, Rose went in search of whiskey.

That night Captain Martin of Gonzales left the fort with a dozen dispatches, including the letter Colonel Travis had drafted three times.

CHAPTER 10

To General Houston, Travis wrote:

"... Today at 10 o'clock A.M. some two or three hundred Mexicans crossed the river below and came up under the houses until they arrived within point blank shot, when we opened a heavy discharge of grape and canister on them, together with well directed fire from small arms which forced them to halt and take shelter in the houses some 90 or 100 yards from our batteries. The action continued to rage about two hours, when the enemy retreated in confusion, dragging off many of their dead and wounded. ... We know from actual observation that many of the enemy were wounded, while we on our part have not lost a man. ... I take great pleasure in stating that both officers and men conducted themselves with firmness and bravery. ..."

He had sent two more couriers east since Bonham's return. After he finished writing his letter to General Houston, Travis paused to consider what Lieutenant Dickerson had said about dispatching so many men from the fort.

He sealed the dispatch. Communications with Houston and the Governor had to be maintained at all costs. They were the only people in Texas with authority enough to rally men and send them to the Alamo.

Billy Wells and Wilson had carried more earth and two mattresses from a storeroom to the roof of the west barracks, and now they had comfortable nests behind little parapets of dirt-filled cowhides. All along the roof and on other buildings men had followed their example.

"This ain't too bad a war," Wells observed.

"If we had more chickens, yeah. I ain't much for that tough beef and half-cooked corn every meal."

"We could sneak into Bexar tonight. I know right where there's a hen house that I was aiming to clean out anyway when things got a little worse."

Half seriously, they considered the idea. It wouldn't take much doing to get into the town, that was a fact, and Wells said he could go straight to the hen house in question with no trouble.

"I dunno," Wilson said. "You take a damn chicken—he squawks his head off at nothing. I can just see ourselves skedaddling for the river, with our arms full of squawking chickens, and Mexican sentries shooting at us every jump."

"Hell, you stick their heads under their wings when you lift 'em off the roost, and then you slip 'em in a sack real quiet-like and they never make a sound."

"You sound like you know the business, right enough!" Wilson laughed. "Every chicken I ever tried to pick up yelled bloody murder."

"We'll get a goat then."

"They blat their heads off. I reckon I can get along on beef and corn for a spell yet."

"Me too, I guess." Wells frowned. "Anyway, the Mexican soldiers probably got them chickens by now."

They watched the flight of a cannonball from the roof of San Fernando Cathedral. It was a long shot and a light battery that the Mexicans had hoisted up there. The ball came in and banged off the base of the wall.

77

The two batteries that the eighteen-pounder had knocked out temporarily resumed their fire, explosive shells that made no impression on the west wall, except to knock off scabs of plaster and leave black sunbursts.

"Why do they keep wastin' their powder like that?" Wilson said.

"They likely got plenty of it."

That day they had seen another cavalry regiment and three battalions of infantry come snaking off the brown hills to reinforce the army already in Bexar.

"A power of the buggers, ain't they?" Wells had said. "Well, just wait till we get *our* reinforcements!"

Major Jameson caught up with Travis in the church when the Colonel was shouting up an order to Jake Walker of Nacogdoches, a gunner on the twelve-pounders.

"We ain't got no explodin' stuff or any of those cans of little balls for these guns," Walker said.

"I know that. What I want you to do is rustle up a few buckets of something that will do, scraps of iron, bent nails—anything you can ram down the muzzle."

Walker scratched his neck. He was a strong, mild-faced man who looked like he didn't belong in the business of war. "Yeah—well, all right, Colonel Travis," he said.

Travis turned to Jameson. "Green?"

Jameson pointed at the scaffold overhead. "We've got to do something about that. It isn't fit to hold a man, and we may need a whole lot of men up there before this is over."

Travis nodded. He hadn't had any more rest than any other officer, which was very little, but yet he looked fit and alert. "What do you suggest?"

"Just what the Mexicans tried today, to wreck some of those *jacals* and bring the wood into the fort."

Travis grinned. "We'll do it!"

He bounced away with characteristic energy to get the operation planned. Major Jameson watched him with a touch of envy. Jameson was tired, and thinking of all the details that still needed to be done to bring the Alamo to a condition that would make it worthy to be called a fort made him more weary.

He went out to get work underway on an inner defense. If the walls were breached, a barricade of dirt fifteen or twenty feet from the first barrier would serve most useful to repel

78

rushes. If it ever came to that, however. . . . He didn't let himself dwell on the thought.

By evening the word was around. A detachment was to sally out that night, tear down some of the huts, get all the wood they could carry away, and kill all the Mexican soldiers they could shoot.

Lieutenant Sam Evans, a Kentuckian, was to lead the raid, for that was what it became in the minds of everyone who wanted to go. Colonel Bonham was assigned to lead a scouting party in advance of the main group to make sure that the raiders didn't run into an ambush.

At midnight Lieutenant Evans assembled his group near the main gate in the south wall. He stood on a tub to look over the shadowy figures. "There's more than fifteen men here."

Muted laughter came from the detail. "Some of us couldn't sleep," a deep voice said.

"I want to look for my watch out there. I lost it when we come to the fort."

"You never had a watch, and you couldn't read it if you did, Coon."

"Quiet, quiet!" Evans said, as laughter ran through the group. "Now listen to me. Bonham has already taken the scouts out. Including him, that's four men. We've got a sentinel about fifty yards out from the southwest corner of the wall.

"I don't want anyone running into him and cutting him loose from his gizzard in the dark. He'll be lying down in a little pit."

"Is it all right to steal his rifle gun?" someone asked, and once more Evans had to quiet laughter.

"You fellows listen to the man." That was Crockett. Everyone turned to peer toward him in the dark.

"Got yer fiddle with you, Davy?" someone asked, but thereafter there was quiet as Evans explained what they were to do.

"The main thing is getting wood for fires and to fix up the platform in the church," Evans said. "Of course, if anyone tries to stop us, we'll do something about it. Remember now, there's four scouts ahead of you, and the sentry that I mentioned."

They went over the barricade and grouped outside. "Easy now," Lieutenant Evans said. "Just follow me."

Probing in advance in the scout detail, John McGregor and

79

Mark Hawkins came silently around opposite sides of a *jacal* and almost ran into each other.

"Bloody hell!" Hawkins whispered, lowering his tomahawk. "Don't be doing that!"

"I've always wanted to kill me an Irishman," McGregor said. He put his knife away.

They stood listening to the night. Bonham was somewhere off to the left, and the other scout was off to the right.

Between the *jacals* they could see dim lights in Bexar, and on the hills to the right there were watchfires of the Mexican army. The night was blacker than a wolf's mouth. Ahead, the *jacals* were deathly quiet.

McGregor touched Hawkins' arm. "Split a little."

They crept on ahead, listening at the wall of each hut for the sounds of breathing or any sound at all that would indicate it was occupied by soldiers.

Each time he passed a *jacal* and had to turn his back on the dark doorway, McGregor felt his flesh crawling. You never could be sure that there hadn't been someone in it.

Like a moor it was, where ghostly figures moved, not quite seen, but sensed. He heard a slight noise behind him somewhere. He swung around quickly, kneeling. Hawkins slid along the wall of a shack and came over to him.

"Don't breathe so loud!" McGregor whispered.

" 'Tis yer own breath you hear, McGregor."

They both heard the faint sounds near the *jacals* they had passed.

"That'll be the byes comin' to get the wood," Hawkins said.

It was, for soon they heard ripping and crashing sounds as the detail began to wreck *jacals*. With that going on, the two scouts knew they had to get far on ahead in order to hear any evidence of a counter-raid by the Mexican forces. They stayed together now.

They were halfway to the river, crouched by a *jacal* that sent an odor to high heaven, as if it held a dead pig, when they heard the murmur of voices ahead of them.

"Sure, and we have some visitors now," Hawkins said.

Shadowy figures loomed up suddenly close ahead. McGregor fired. He heard Hawkins' rifle crack. A voice cried out in pain. Muskets boomed, making great orange blossoms. McGregor heard a ball whisk through the straw roof of the *jacal* where he crouched, reloading.

An instant later two more rifles cracked, off to the right

80

and on the left. Bonham and the other scout. McGregor had just finished reloading when he saw the pale uniform pantaloons of an infantryman right in front of him. He fired without aiming. The men grunted and then he was down, moaning.

McGregor was tugging at his pistol, too late, when he saw the second soldier. Then there was a sharp chop as Hawkins swung his tomahawk. The soldier crashed against the corner of the *jacal* and fell at MGregor's feet.

"Back!" McGregor said.

They withdrew slowly, hearing the scrape of rawhide sandals advancing toward them. By crouching they could see along the ground and make out the lightness of the pantaloons above the sandals. McGregor put a bullet from his pistol just above the paleness. He heard the heavy impact of it and the soldier grunted.

For an instant McGregor thought they had been caught from behind, when the musket belched a few feet from him.

"Christ!" Hawkins said. "What do they load these things with?" He dropped the musket he had fired, the piece he had snatched from the ground back there where he had killed its owner with the tomahawk.

Balls were ripping through the flimsy *jacals* around them as McGregor and Hawkins withdrew again. They nearly ran into a tall figure, who said, "Don't hurry, boys."

Crockett had come up with part of the work crew.

The spiteful crack of long rifles, some of them with blobs of cotton on the front sight, drove the Mexicans back. From *jacal* to *jacal* the thin line of Americans advanced, firing only when they saw the paleness of uniforms.

Lieutenant Evans called, "Colonel Crockett, send some of those men back here. We've got work to do!"

Presently the wrecking of the *jacals* was resumed, while part of the detail stayed out on the skirmish line. "They're like Indians," Crockett said, "they got no stomach for night fighting." He was standing up, and the scrape of his ramrod said that he was reloading. "Come on, boys, let's go up ahead and look around."

The skirmish line advanced. Off to the left a cannon was firing as fast as the gunners could service it, but all the balls were passing high overhead, some of them making orange-colored bursts on the walls of the Alamo.

On toward the river the skirmish line advanced, firing when they saw targets. McGregor fell over the dirt of a newly-dug entrenchment and landed on a wounded Mexican, who murmured a plea in Spanish. McGregor leaped away quickly from him, feeling the stickiness of blood on his hand. He knelt and scrubbed it off in the dirt.

The firing ahead grew heavier and the flashes indicated a solid line along some barrricade or entrenchment. "I reckon we've traveled far enough for one night," Crockett said. "Let's saunter back."

Each time he spoke they knew by the sound of his voice that he was standing erect, as unconcerned by the firing ahead as he had been in daytime on the walls of the Alamo.

With a man like Crockett, you could go a long way, McGregor thought. You felt better when he was around.

The skirmish line fell back. McGregor stepped on a dead man and jumped aside with a startled grunt. "What's the matter?" Hawkins asked.

When McGregor told him, the Irishman laughed. "Yer skittish, me bye. 'Tis the live ones that you want to be fearful of."

McGregor had his revenge later when Hawkins' feet brushed against the legs of a dead soldier. "Mother of Christ!" the Irishman yelped, and dropped some of the looted muskets he was carrying.

Round on round the battery to the southwest kept firing, until the cannoneers stopped to let the piece cool. "A thing like that could disturb yer sleep, I'm thinking," Hawkins said to McGregor. "But I suppose a Scotsman wouldn't care, since he stays up all night anyway counting his money."

"Noo, noo, lad!" McGregor answered. "They oft stay up all night, true, but merely to count the scalps of the Irishmen taken that day in fair combat."

About a hundred paces from the *jacals* that Lieutenant Evans' men were tearing down, Crockett set up a picket line, but except for the battery that fired intermittently there was no further effort to drive the Americans from their work, so after a time they left only a few men on picket duty and gathered timber with a will.

Some of those inside the Alamo, who had been roused by the brisk little firefight, and then kept awake by the Mexican battery, came out to help carry boards and poles into the fort.

By dawn the Americans had retired into the Alamo, with enough wood to keep their cooking fires supplied for several days, and enough material to make a stout platform inside the church.

Jim Bowie was on his feet, with a few good words to say for their efforts. Now and then he had been showing himself around the fort, encouraging the volunteers, but he never stayed up long, and it didn't take a doctor to know that he was bad sick.

As usual, Travis was in high spirits. That his men, outnumbered as they were, could sally forth, kill some of the enemy and supply themselves with wood, all without the loss of a man, was a signal mark of the superiority of the army under his command.

Though Travis was elated, there were others who looked soberly at a few basic facts. Dickerson and Blazeby stood on the south barracks and observed the marks that sappers had made during the night.

To the south, about three hundred yards away, a battery was well-seated behind an earthen embankment, and there was another one off to the southwest, much farther away. Both of them were firing. They were light and they were doing no great damage, but both the officers knew that the batteries, and others, might be moved a little closer when night came.

They were not students of classical siege war, but the facts were obvious: Santa Anna's men were not obliged to rush the Alamo. They could keep constricting their grip around it, hammering and battering, wearing the defenders down.

Unless reinforcements came, there could be only one ending.

The brass four-pounders behind the lunette, outside the porte-cochere at the south end of the fort, were replying to the nearest battery, but the dirt embankment protecting the enemy gun was sponging up the light shot. Even as Blazeby and Dickerson watched, the two four-pounders gave up.

Blazeby eyed a ball coming from the battery to the southwest. With deceptive slowness it curved through the crisp morning air. He said, "It looks like you could almost catch that in your hands, doesn't it?"

Dickerson nodded. "I wouldn't advise it, though." And then almost in the same breath he asked, "When did the last courier go out?"

"Yesterday. It was yesterday, wasn't it?"

"Seems like it was. It's hard to remember time when day and night run together."

They looked at the Mexican cavalry encamped on the hills

east and northeast of the Alamo. They were having morning muster over there. A bugle call came clearly. The Mexican Colors made a bright flutter.

"Watch that one!" Dickerson warned, grabbing Blazeby's arm.

A ball was coming straight at them and it appeared that it would reach the barracks, but it fell short as they dropped to the roof. Small rocks and earth fell on them in a shower.

They stood up again and the men near them rose.

"We're bound to get reinforcements," Blazeby said.

"Of course we will."

"What was it Bonham said—that Colonel Fannin had at least five hundred men at Goliad?"

"Close to that," Dickerson said. "They should be rallying to him every day. You can bet that General Houston isn't going to stand around idly when he knows what's going on here. It'll take a little time for them to get organized, I suppose, supplies and all of that."

Standing nearby, Louis Rose thought: They talk for the men to hear, or for themselves? Reinforcement, yes. It was possible. As a trader, one who had seen much of the people of the Texas colonies, Rose knew that they helped each other in many ways, when they weren't quarrelling or fighting.

Although he knew more of a soldier's life than anyone within the Alamo, it was not as a soldier that Rose was here. He had come to Bexar on business and now he was trapped.

Although there had been little fighting, already he had seen with his own eyes enough of the besieging army to gauge the temper of it.

The uniforms were fine, yes, and the cavalry rode well, but the Mexican army was not like the English he had fought, disciplined and steady; nor like the Austrians, grim and fierce; nor like the regiments of Saxons, wild as Indians, those stubborn Saxons who had turned back Caesar himself.

But the Mexican army was good enough. It was of no importance to say it was not the best army in the world, for if they killed you—that was enough for any army to do.

All this brave talk and laughter about the wood that had been secured. Poof! There should be some concern about those batteries that had been placed while a little wood-stealing was going on. To be sure, the guns were doing no damage now, but tomorrow they would be closer and there would be more of them.

If they only made noise, that would be bad enough, for the constant crashing of cannons was more than sufficient to make men nervous, even one's own cannons, and when men were nervous they did strange things and were not themselves.

But perhaps it was so . . . reinforcements would come.

To settle his own nerves Rose went to find Jim Garrand, who spoke excellent French, and who had yet some wine in a jug concealed behind loose stones in the north wall.

CHAPTER 11

SINCE HE WAS a sergeant, Panfilio Olid had more experience lying to his superiors than ordinary soldiers, and so, showing great concern for the welfare of his men, he told his captain that he must go to Bexar to obtain medicine for Dragoon Felix Galan, who was near death from a bellyache caused from drinking bad water on the way from Laredo.

Since Panfilio was a good sergeant, Captain Ramon Condille suffered the lie patiently, and let him go to Bexar, where Panfilio promptly found his old friend Veedor Bustamente.

They soon made it Gonzalo's turn to suffer; drinking his wine, recalling old times at a table in the cantina; and Gonzalo knew that because of his friendship for a friend of his grandfather's whom he had never seen before, he would not be paid for the wine.

Indeed these revolutions were monstrous calamities.

After Veedor had fondly recalled all the bad things he could remember of Panfilio, and Panfilio had agreed on every point, the two arrived at the present situation in Bexar.

"The infantry." Veedor shook his head. "It is not good."

"All infantry is worthless," said Panfilio. "We sit on a hill to keep them from running away."

"So few women with the army this time."

"They died walking the deserts and the uplands and on the way from Laredo. There are not three hundred left." Panfilio shrugged and called for more wine.

"No padres in this army?" Veedor asked. "I saw none. We always had padres in the old days."

"That was the Spanish influence, Don Bustamente. There is

no padre with us and no doctor. We have something greater—Santa Anna."

They looked at each other with understanding, with sly laughter in their eyes, and drank their wine, while Gonzalo, whose ears hung low, shuddered at such dangerous talk.

"Last night this great one went to the meeting of the Masons in Lieutenant Hernandez' tent," Panfilio said. "It was Mexican Rites, they say, although the great one is of the Scottish Rites, and before that of the York, it is said."

"That is understandable," Veedor nodded solemnly. "He *must* go to know what the young officers are plotting."

They both laughed.

"And the battle," Veedor said, "how does that go?"

Panfilio shrugged. "The *zapadores* dig by night. Sometimes the North Americans come out and shoot at them, and then the *zapadores* run, but they always go back and dig again."

This was what Bernal had said also. Bernal was very busy going from gun to gun, selling little cakes and tortillas to those who had money to buy, and seeing everything that he could. He knew much of what was going on, but nothing of Jim Bowie, and this was troubling Veedor.

"Big Jim, we have not heard of him since the battle started," Veedor said. "What do you hear, Panfilio?"

Panfilio shrugged. "That is strange. He has not been seen on the walls. Perhaps he is dead. The big loud one is there always, the one in the animal hat, who kills officers a mile away."

"Crockett," said Veedor, with as much accuracy as any Mexican could say the name.

"That is the one." Panfilio frowned. "Sometimes I think he does not kill enough officers."

"This would not apply, of course, to sergeants?"

"No, no! Mainly to lieutenants and generals."

The army had not changed in some respects, Veedor was pleased to know. "But no one has seen Big Jim?"

Panfilio shook his head. "He has been killed."

"This cannot be so. I do not believe it."

Panfilio shrugged. "I must return now. This afternoon some of the cavalry will go east to fight the North Americans coming from Goliad."

"They are coming?"

"It has been said. I do not know."

After he had listened, without hearing, to Gonzalo's groaning about the amount of wine Panfilio Olid had consumed,

Veedor rose and went outside, wobbling a little because of his knees and the wine he too had drunk.

Jim Bowie could not be dead. It was impossible. Wounded, yes. That was it! He had been wounded, and now something should be done to cheer him, to let him know that his old friend was thinking of him.

Veedor dozed, waiting. His head bobbed in little jerks each time a cannon fired. He roused when he heard Bernal's bare feet slapping the earth close by.

"Bernal!"

"Yes, Grandfather." The boy came over and stood before Veedor, scratching mightily.

With one eye on the doorway of the cantina, where Big Ears might pop out any moment, Veedor talked softly, telling Bernal what he wished him to do that night.

"Tonight?"

"Yes!"

Bernal's eyes were big with thinking. He kept scratching with both hands. He grinned. "I will do that."

"You won't have hands for it if you scratch so." Veedor frowned. "What is consuming you?"

"We climbed a tree by the river, Juan Diaz and I, to watch the cannons fire at the fort. There was a nest of birds and from them lice came and crawled upon us."

"Ten million of them, it would seem."

From the back wall of the church, Travis stared east to where a troop of cavalry was encamped astride the Gonzales road. "They need to be knocked around a little," he growled. "They're too damn' smug and sure of themselves."

Captain Despallier's eyes began to gleam, but he said carefully, "What good would a sally do?"

"They're sitting right on the route our reinforcements will use. I'd like them to realize that we're capable of hitting them from the fort."

"That might make them increase their force out there."

"Good! That will leave a hole somewhere else for our men to come through."

Despallier volunteered on the spot to lead a sally against the Mexican horse. He picked sixteen men, though everyone who had a mount fit to ride wanted to go.

As the column picked up to a fast trot on the way across

the plain, Private Richard Starr shouted across to Dan Bourne, "What are we supposed to do, now that we're about to do it?"

Bourne grinned. "We raise some hell with 'em and come scooting back, I reckon."

Despallier, who liked to ride like the devil was on his tail, looked back at his company. The column of fours was already coming apart as some men tried to surge ahead and others swung right or left to avoid dust. No matter, Despallier thought, this wasn't a review.

He let out a yell and waved them on. What was left of the formation broke apart entirely, scattering into a line of wild, yelling riders.

Thunder of hoofs. The brims of tight-pulled hats flopping in the wind. Yowls and Indian whoops and cattle yells. The sixteen men raced out as if they were going to trample the cavalry camp ahead and chase the survivors all the way to the Gulf.

The Mexican camp watched them with mild surprise for a while, a handful of ragged men charging like they owned the earth. Only a few of the Mexicans were mounted, couriers standing ready to carry dispatches to other units of the army sprawled around the hard walls of the Alamo.

Half the horses were in a rope corral, unsaddled.

"Come on, ride!" Despallier yelled. It appeared that they could catch the camp in confusion, and then he saw the Mexicans moving swiftly as officers shouted orders.

Before the Americans had covered half the distance to the camp, red-coated riders had formed up hastily. Lancer pennons fluttered and the Mexicans came out to meet the enemy.

"Carry through one time!" Despallier yelled.

His men knew what he meant, meet the first shock, go through and turn, and then ride back out of the confusion, knocking over any red coat that was handy.

The two lines crashed together. Dan Bourne saw a lance leveled at his chest, a white-toothed brown face looking down it. He fired his pistol and missed, and then he swung out in the saddle. The lance went by, but the shock of the horses coming together knocked Bourne's gray into a staggering spin that threw him from the saddle.

He lit on his hands and knees, his pistol gone. The gray swung clear around, dragging him by the reins before it could stop. He looked straight into the Mexican camp for an instant. Men were running, shouting, saddling horses.

Behind him was dust and fierce shouts, the roar of pistols, the pounding of hoofs, but for a moment he seemed all alone in the fight, stretched out on the ground, hanging to the reins with both hands as his horse sidled.

He had just retrieved his empty pistol when he heard Despallier's shout, "Back! Back!"

Bourne grabbed the horn and mounted as the gray tried to swing away from him. He was confused for a moment as to which way to go, and then he heard Despallier's shout again. As he spurred through the plunging dust he saw Starr ahead of him, grappling with a Mexican lancer.

Bourne came in from the back and clubbed the Mexican with his pistol as he rode by. The man slumped over his horse's neck and Starr almost fell out of the saddle as the lance he had been struggling for came free.

"Back to the fort, Dick!" Bourne yelled, and Starr looked at him blankly, though he swung his horse and rode, carrying the lance.

Bourne's horse grunted as it leaped a dead red-coated body, and then he was clear, racing back toward the Alamo. A ragged line of American riders was there ahead of him, shouting defiance as they rode.

Starr came up beside Bourne, waving the lance. "Look what I got!"

"I ought to know. I helped you get it!"

"Like hell you did!" Starr said, and from his expression Bourne knew that he didn't, and perhaps never would, realize how he had got that lance.

Behind them, the Mexicans, though badly mauled by the sharp and unexpected encounter, had regrouped and were coming after the retreating Americans, and in their lead was a big sergeant who rode like he was going to fall from his horse at every leap.

Rifles on the chapel and along the east wall of the convent yard began to spit. Horses veered away and went trotting across the plain after their red-coated riders fell from them.

The twelve-pounder that pointed east in the chapel, the only piece in all the Alamo that was pointed in that direction, boomed, and the Americans heard the *whush* of a ball passing overhead. It also passed above the heads of the pursuing cavalry, who were already breaking speed and veering away under the deadly rifle fire.

And then they broke entirely and rode back toward their

89

camp, with the big, clumsy-riding sergeant the last to give up.

Screaming like fiends and riding like Comanches, the Americans pounded back to the Alamo. The main gate was thrown open to them, but only two riders followed Despallier inside.

Starr waved his captured lance and yelled, "Once around the fort, boys, for the hell of it!"

No sooner said than they were off. They hadn't lost a man in their brief encounter with the cavalry and their appetite for raising hell was whetted.

They raced out from the east wall, while Mexican batteries sent dirt flying at their heels. When they turned the corner at the north end of the wall, musket fire came at them from nearby *jacals*. Starr waved the lance and yelled.

With one accord the riders charged the *jacals*. A few infantrymen ran from the houses, their long-tailed blue coats flying as they retreated toward entrenchments two hundred yards away.

"By God, let's clean out some of these shacks!" Bill Cummings suggested.

"Get some wood while you're out there!" came a long call from someone on the north wall.

The raiders dismounted and began to tear down the *jacals* where the infantrymen had been taking cover. Someone ran forward and fired the straw roof of a house, and then ran back as a steady fire developed from the entrenchments.

Travis saw what was happening. He called for more riflemen on the north wall. They were already on their way. As the Mexican infantry came out of the entrenchments and began an advance, he ordered the three eight-pounders facing north to fire.

The guns roared and bucked back against their trails. One of them was loaded with scraps of iron and pieces of broken jugs that screamed and whirred as they cut through the ragged lines of advancing soldiers.

Riflemen began to take their toll, but the Mexicans came on, taking cover behind *jacals*.

Then Travis sent men over the walls to help carry back wood. Starr had driven his lance into the ground and tied his horse to it. A Texan started to carry the lance away and there was a loud, profane argument that lasted until Starr snatched it back from him. "I captured that!" Starr shouted. "Nobody's going to make firewood out of my lance!"

In the face of stiff opposition from the steadily reinforced infantry, the raiders managed to get a great many cedar planks from some of the *jacals*. Men trotted back with them and handed them up to eager hands on the north wall.

"Cavalry!" Bourne shouted.

A column was coming from the northeast.

The Americans scrambled back to their horses, just as a heavy, crackling fire broke out all along the north wall. Once more a column of Mexican horsemen broke and swung away under the deadly accuracy of the riflemen.

From the chapel the twelve-pounder pointing north sent a futile ball after them as they rode away.

It was then that Bourne saw the horse with the silver-mounted saddle. It was trotting toward the corner of the cattle pen, throwing its head to keep from stepping on its bridle reins.

Bourne went streaking toward it, grabbed the reins and in triumph towed it around the fort and into the gate. A few minutes later the other raiders, thumbing their noses at the Mexican cannon fire, galloped around the east side of the Alamo and entered the plaza.

Though he had been disturbed at first by their unpremeditated sortie against the *jacals*, Colonel Travis, whose commission was cavalry, came forward to congratulate the riders.

"You'd think they'd trompled the whole Mexican army, from the way he's carrying on," Tapley Holland told a companion as they listened to Travis from the top of the chapel.

"They did make it hot out there for a while, you got to admit."

When he went back to his post on the north wall, Starr set the butt of the lance firmly into a crack in the masonry. The pennon streamed out and there the trophy stood for Santa Anna's men to see. "That'll remind 'em that we'll fight on the outside as well as from the fort," Starr said.

The sortie by the Texas cavalry raised the spirits of the whole garrison. Though the cannon fire never ceased, the defenders of the Alamo had learned to live with it, even when shells cleared the walls and exploded in the plaza, or burst resoundingly on the stout stone walls of the buildings.

During the daytime, those on the walls could see the balls coming and yell a warning when it appeared that one of them was going to drop inside. By night, men took the chance that any stray ball would not fall near them, if they wished to cross the plaza.

91

A rifle ball, they reasoned, was far more dangerous than a cannon ball.

And so no one appeared to pay any great attention to the Mexican artillery that night after the cavalry raid when men gathered to hear the concert. Davy Crockett's long, gaunt face grinned above the fiddle he was sawing, while John McGregor, who preferred to be called Ben, accompanied him with the bagpipes.

They were standing near a fire at the southwest corner of the fort. Dick Stockton, one of the youngest fighters in the Alamo, warmed his hands as he held his long rifle between his knees. "Old Davy's playing 'Rory O'Moore'," he said, cocking his head, "but what's McGregor blowing on that pig's bladder?"

"That's no pig's bladder, lad," said Bob Campbell, outraged. "Ben's playing the marching song of the McGregors."

"I don't know what it is, but I sure as hell knew they wasn't playing the same song."

The pipes shrilled louder and louder and McGregor began to move his feet. Though Crockett struggled valiantly, he was losing ground, and at last he lowered his fiddle and looked around with a grin.

"That fellow ought to be in Congress," he announced. "With all the wind he's got, he could win every argument that came up!"

Crouched in the dark outside the walls, on lonely sentinel duty, the outposts heard the sounds inside and felt not quite so alone.

And Mexican *zapadores* creeping along the ditch behind the walls of the church, on a mission to determine the easiest place to shut off the water, heard the outlandish music and the laughter of the North Americans and wondered what kind of people they were to take war so lightly.

CHAPTER 12

BY THE MAIN GATE, Pete Bailey leaned against the wall of the barracks and dozed, standing on his feet. It was darker than the belly of a cow, and the night was chill. Two hours before he had let a courier out, and that was about all that was going on tonight, except that damned cannon fire that never ended.

Bailey roused when his head jerked forward. He walked along the wall of the barracks and came back to his post, but a few moments later he felt himself dozing again.

He didn't know how long it was before he heard the soft voice calling, "Bowie, Bowie!" He roused with a start and swung his rifle toward the gate.

"Who's there?"

"Bowie. Big Jim!"

Like hell it is, Bailey thought, and then he came fully awake. He was standing right against a crack in the log-reinforced planks of the gate. Somebody could've rammed a bayonet through there and spitted him like a piece of roasting meat.

He jumped back and cocked his rifle. "Who's there?"

"Bernal Bustamente." The voice ran on in Spanish.

"Why, it's just a kid!" But who was out there with him? Bailey wasn't about to open any gate.

Crockett loomed up suddenly in the dark, walking soundlessly in his moccasins. "What's all the infernal yelling and shooting about, Pete?"

"I didn't shoot. There's a Mexican kid out there."

"What's he want?"

"Bowie, Bowie!" Bernal whispered loudly.

Crockett disappeared into the dark. Bailey heard a light thump as he went over the barricade, and presently he returned with a Mexican boy in tow. "He's got a bottle of something with him. Now that's the kind of man we need more of!"

Captain Forsyth came over to the gate. "What's going on here?"

"A friend of Bowie's, looks like," Crockett said.

Forsyth peered hard. "Why, he could be a spy!"

"Aw, hell," said Crockett, and led Bernal over to the headquarters room, and there in the dim light Bernal held up the bottle of white rum he carried and managed to explain why he had come.

"I wish I had a few friends like him out there," Crockett said. "Come on, boy."

"You're not going to disturb Colonel Bowie at this hour?"

"He won't mind, even if he's asleep, which I doubt."

93

Jim Bowie was not asleep. His man, Ham, was wrapped in a blanket and snoring on the floor beside Bowie's cot.

"Big Jim!" Bernal cried, and trotted forward with his gift.

Bowie's fevered eyes looked at the boy blankly for a moment, and then he smiled and struggled to sit up. "Take it easy-like there," Crockett said, and gave Bowie a hand, and then the Tennessean turned and walked out of the room.

Bernal left a half hour later. Bailey escorted him over the barricade, shaking his head as the boy disappeared quietly into the darkness.

The crumping roar of the artillery went on all night long.

Near dawn Bernal crept into the room of his great-grandfather, where the old man was making soft grunting noises as he slept on the stove-top. Bernal hesitated a moment, then shook him gently.

Veedor was awake instantly.

Tears streaked through the grime on Bernal's face as he said, "He is dying! Jim Bowie is dying!"

The old man grabbed his shoulder with a hand like a talon. "This cannot be."

"It is so," the lad blubbered. He told what he had seen, and in the telling, because it was quite easy to confuse the things Bowie had said, Bernal said that Big Jim had been struck by a cannon ball while standing on the wall of the Alamo.

Veedor sat in silence with his aching legs hanging over the edge of the stove. The years were very heavy on him. Another of the great ones gone, and by the hand of a despot, perhaps the worst of them all.

Systems of government, dictatorships, or republics such as the *tejanos* talked about, were only words to Veedor Bustamente. One loved or hated men, not endless words that tried to explain the actions of men.

And now Veedor's hatred of Santa Anna was even blacker than it had been before. If he didn't have so many years . . . but no, perhaps it was not just the years and the agony of his knees, but fear and laziness that made him do nothing but gossip like a woman and be unreasonable with his only grandson, worthless as the grandson was.

Perhaps there was yet honor and courage in his heart, and if it was there, the body would have to follow.

"Go, Bernal. Say nothing of this."

At dawn the Mexican artillery fire increased, as gunners who had slept all night replaced those who had served the batteries during the dark hours. The big gun of the Alamo boomed out, carrying its sound far across the hills and plains, the morning signal that the Alamo still stood.

Inside the walls there was no relief for those who had stood the watch the night before, because now the defenders were working feverishly to build inner lines of barricades, earthworks near the north wall, a place to fall back to in case the outer wall was breached.

And inside each doorway of the long, two-story barracks along the east wall they were building barriers of earth-filled cowhides that were lashed to poles set in the ground. From those curving defenses, breast-high, riflemen could cover the doorways, obliquely and straight ahead.

In one of the rooms One-Eye Guerrero paused in his work to sight his rifle above the barrier. He swung the weapon in an arc and his single eye squinted evilly as he sighted toward the doorway.

Private George Pagan said, "I don't much like this business."

Andres Nava grinned. "What do you mean?"

"Making these things sort of smells like somebody was figuring we was going to be trapped in here."

"That is true," One-Eye said. "Is not this a better place to die than being dragged on a rope by cavalry while running to escape?" He squinted down his rifle, smiling.

Pagan dropped his shovel and walked outside. By God, no, it wasn't a better place to die. As far as he was concerned, no place was a good spot for dying. In fact, he just didn't figure on dying at all.

He went back and got his shovel and took it over toward the north wall where they were digging. It was a better place to work, where nobody was talking about dying.

Dickerson and Lieutenant Robert Evans, master of ordnance, watched newly-seated Mexican batteries from a gun platform near the north wall. From the old mill north of them an eight-pounder was heaving solid shot at the wall. From behind a high burm on the old *acequia* that ran the length of the west wall, another battery was dug in, much closer than the first.

"What day is this?" Dickerson asked suddenly.

Evans frowned. "The twenty-seventh, or twenty-eighth? I've

lost track." He was a tall, black-haired man, generally full of laughter, but now his face showed tenseness and his blue eyes were bloodshot from lack of sleep. "It must be the twenty-eighth, at least."

They watched a ball from the eight-pounder come in and strike with a solid smash against the wall. Masonry fell from the top. The ditch battery fired. Dust hung lazy in the air after the projectile hit the wall.

"Who went out last night besides Bonham?" Evans asked.

"Despallier."

"Where to this time?"

"Despallier went to Gonzales to hurry reinforcements along."

"Yeah," Evans said doubtfully. "That makes about fifteen couriers who were going to hurry reinforcements from some place. What happens to them?"

"It takes time to get men together. You know that."

They both looked toward the east.

Quiet lay the land out there, no dust to indicate the approach of a relief force, no activity from the enemy horses. Uncertainty, emptiness and waiting.

If they knew that help was on the way, it would make the waiting easier, Evans thought; but they did not know what was happening to their couriers. Relief would come, but when? Behind that last thought was a greater worry that Evans didn't care to say aloud: Suppose no help at all came to the Alamo?

The artillery kept beating at the walls. They were still largely intact but they couldn't stand forever the constant hammering by day and night.

Only occasionally were the guns within the fort replying. Powder was running low. Evans was well aware of other disturbing facts about the ordnance, too. Aside from Hutchinson on the eighteen-pounder, no one knew how to sight the pieces skillfully. The seating of the guns on the dirt platforms restricted their field of fire.

All this ran through Lieutenant Evans' mind as he stared off to the east, toward Goliad and Gonzales, the nearest places from which relief could come.

Someone yelled, "There comes a high one!"

An instant later there came the crump of one of the howitzers near the river, about a five-incher, Evans estimated. The ball sailed high, carried over the west wall and bounced in the middle of the plaza without exploding.

One-Eye Guerrero, his big hat flopping as he ran, rushed from the west barracks and began to cover the missile with dirt. A cannoneer from the four-pound batteries behind the south barricade ran up and began to kick the dirt away, arguing that he wanted the ball to use against infantry.

"She no blow up one time," Guerrero said. "What's the good?"

"I can use it," the cannoneer said, and walked off juggling the ball from hand to hand.

Private Hawkins called up to Evans, "Lieutenant, can I have some powder?"

"What for?"

"I've an idea for making me some bombs to tickle the toes of the enemy."

Evans walked down the ramp. "I can't spare any good powder, but there's some old stuff the Mexicans left here that I'll give you."

"Just so it blows up, Lieutenant."

"It'll burn, but that's about all."

They started toward the church. "What do you have in mind?" Evans asked.

"I captured some muskets when we went out to get wood, and now I want to see if I can make long bombs out of them."

Evans grinned at the apt description.

In the sacristy of the church, while Hawkins held a candle and stayed near the doorway, Evans scooped a few handfuls of loose powder onto an old piece of canvas. He made a rough sack of the canvas and gave it to Hawkins, whose eyes had narrowed at what he'd seen in the magazine.

"What's the matter with that Mexican powder?" he asked.

"General Cos left it here last winter. It's been wet and it's full of dirt and some thieving contractor diluted it with too much charcoal in the first place."

When Hawkins climbed up to the roof of the west barracks with two clattering Mexican muskets, his powder and his own armament, Ben McGregor shook his head. "Noo, I suppose you're going to kill Santa Anna himself, at a thousand yards, with those smoothbores."

"I'm going to do better than that, lad. I'm about to build some lovely bombs to kill off all the Scotsmen fighting in the Mexican army."

"No such thing!"

Hawkins sat down on the roof with his plunder. He tried a

97

few pinches of the powder. It burned slowly, sputtering and smoking a great deal. "You might kill a flea with that," McGregor said, "if you hit him with a rock first."

Billy Wells and Wilson came over, watching with great interest.

"Tread lightly, boys, a great inventor is aboot to give birth to something," McGregor said.

"What is it?" asked Wells.

McGregor spread his hands. "The Lord only knows!"

" 'Tis an ignorant bunch that a man of my great intelligence is forced to associate with," Hawkins said. He rose and removed his coat and spread it on the roof, dumping the powder on it and smoothing it with his hand. "Now, McGregor, be kind enough to pick the bits of dirt from that whilst the sun is drying it—such sun as there is this day."

McGregor put out his hand to comply, and then he withdrew it quickly when he realized that the dirt in the power was even finer than the other elements. Wells and Wilson laughed.

Hawkins hefted one of the *escopetas*. "Now here's the thing of it, byes. In some way I remove the barrel of this beauty, then I choke it full of powder, plug the ends, light the fuse—and there you are."

"Aye!" McGregor said. "With your head blown off."

"You fail to grasp the point, McGregor. It's on the Mexicans below, when they come in against the walls where we can't shoot at them, that I drop the bomb."

"That's good." McGregor nodded. "If it strikes one of them on the head, it may be of some good."

Hawkins frowned at the musket. " 'Tis a fuse that troubles me."

"That's simple," Wells said, sober-faced. "Don't worry about taking the barrel off. You can't anyway. You load the musket clear to the end and then—"

"Now you have an idea!" Hawkins approved.

"You load it tight as she'll go," Wells said. "You don't need worry about a fuse."

"Why not?" Hawkins asked.

"You prime it, pull the trigger, and throw it over the wall as fast as you can."

Hawkins grinned while his companions roared with laughter. "I should have expected such advice," he said.

"High one coming!" Wilson yelled.

They all jerked their heads to watch the howitzer ball. It exploded somewhere in the plaza. As if it were a signal, all the batteries that were steadily inching up on the Alamo began to fire as fast as the gunners could serve the pieces.

"I'm getting just a little weary of all this," Wilson said suddenly.

Wells walked across the roof and stood looking east for a while.

"They'll come, lad," McGregor said. "Don't be worrying, they'll come."

Wilson swept his gaze around the plain. Entrenchments in all directions. Batteries everywhere. More and more soldiers had come marching into Bexar. Santa Anna's headquarters was now on this side of the river. You could tell by the number of couriers constantly coming and going just about where he was located.

"How many are out there?" Wilson asked, of no one in particular.

"It looks like ten thousand," McGregor said. "Divide that by half and maybe you'll have a good guess." He lay back on the roof and closed his eyes.

Wilson walked across the roof and looked east. He saw the hated cavalry, taking their ease, with nothing to do but sit on the road and wait.

Beyond was only land, with a *carreta* crawling slowly eastward.

Sergeant Panfilio Olid went bumping up to headquarters with his dispatch. He looked incuriously at the long line of people waiting to see the Napoleon of the West, old women with their shawls drawn close about their faces, merchants of Bexar, officials of the town dressed in their best clothes, and others come to beg favors of the great one.

Panfilio delivered his dispatch and turned back to his horse, and it was then that he saw Veedor Bustamente in the group of waiting people, standing on stiff-locked legs, his face straight ahead and quiet.

All around were soldiers to see that no one rushed before Santa Anna before first being sharply interviewed by a young lieutenant in a fine, new uniform.

Panfilio led his horse down toward the group.

"Don Bustamente."

Veedor would not look at him.

"Don Bustamente, you are too old to fight North Americans."

And still Veedor looked straight ahead.

Panfilio was very sure then. He began to sweat a little, for the young lieutenant had noticed him, and noticed Veedor too. Panfilio did something then that he did not like to do. He walked into the crowd of patient people and turned Veedor with his hands and made him look.

"Don't touch me with your hands!" Veedor said, and his eyes were black and bitter. He struck Panfilio's arm and turned away again.

And now the lieutenant, slim and straight and with great authority in his manner, came through the crowd without regard for old ones who could not move quickly from his path.

"What passes here?" he asked sharply.

Panfilio saluted his very best. "This old one here, I know him," he said apologetically. "He was in the glorious army long ago and fought most bravely for Mexico, and now—"

"I have no interest in lying tales. What does he wish here?"

"He wishes to fight the North Americans, Lieutenant, but I have tried to—"

"Let *him* speak!"

Veedor was too proud to look at the ground, and he knew he must not let the lieutenant see directly into his eyes, so he looked straight ahead. "I wish to see his Excellency."

"Every whining idiot here has the same wish! I ask why you—"

The lieutenant cursed as someone stumbled against him and stepped on the toe of his beautiful boots. Francisco Ruiz, it seemed, had been jostled by the crowd and thrown off balance. He began to apologize for his clumsiness.

"With your permission, Lieutenant, I would take this old one away. There will be one less to trouble his Excellency," Panfilio said.

The lieutenant was staring with anger at his boot, and it was then that Panfilio picked Veedor up and carried him swiftly from the place. The lieutenant scowled for a moment. There had been something about that old one. . . . Ah, but they were all alike, with their petty woes and complaints and tearful begging for favors.

"You," he said to Ruiz, "will be the very last one to see his Excellency, if I even allow it then."

100

Behind the trees Panfilio put old Veedor down with great gentleness.

"You have insulted me," Veedor said.

"You think they do not search you when you go near Santa Anna? You think you could stand with murder in your eyes and have it not known?"

Veedor's expression changed slowly. "I did not think they would search an old one like me."

Panfilio let out a long sigh. "Everyone among those waiting saw what I saw. The lieutenant's brains may be in his pretty boots, but he would have seen too, had not one of your friends stumbled for no reason!"

"The *alcalde*."

Panfilio put a big hand gently on the old man's shoulder. "You will go home now and put the knife away?"

Veedor nodded. He was thinking on to something else.

"Jim Bowie is dead," he murmured, making a fact of something he sensed within him.

"They all will be dead soon, those in the fort. It is something that we can do nothing about, Don Bustamente. We both have seen such things happen before, many times. You will go home now?"

"I go."

Veedor hobbled away slowly.

His thought is very good, Panfilio told himself as he went to get his horse, but let some wild young officer who screams of liberty and justice in secret meetings do this deed, not those of us who will gain nothing by it.

One who killed a dictator was a great hero, until he in turn became a dictator and was killed by another hero, and from all these events came nothing but evil for those like Panfilio and Veedor and all the other poor people of Mexico. But if one troubled himself about all the unfortunate things that happened constantly, he soon would be so unhappy that he too would be crying liberty and justice!

It was sufficient to be a sergeant of the cavalry. There were enough worries in fighting North Americans who rode like screaming fiends from hell. Panfilio Olid was no coward, and this he knew without having to question himself on the subject, but yet he would be content if the North Americans stayed in the Alamo with what few horses they had, giving no more of their hellish exhibitions outside the fort.

Moving briskly so that he would not be a good target, he

followed around the bend of the San Antonio on his way back to his troop, observing the number of new batteries that had been placed recently, and the advances that others had made.

Dirty from their digging, a group of *zapadores* was marching toward the river with a sergeant. Panfilio observed them with the fine contempt of a cavalryman. Like many of the other foot soldiers, they were poor devils who had been caught out of their little fields and pushed into a uniform and given a musket.

Someday when they had to rush the fort, if the noisy artillery ever made a hole in it, which seemed doubtful, the cavalry would have to stay behind them to keep them from running far away from the deadly fire of the long rifles.

Ah, yes, it was best to be a cavalryman.

Now it was February 29, 1836.

CHAPTER 13

IN SPITE of the cannonading Dan Bourne barely managed to stay awake until he was relieved at his post on a firing ramp at the north wall. He went dragging away with no desire except to stumble into the barracks and fall on his blankets.

But there was something he had to do first. He had prevailed upon the cooks to issue his supper ration of corn before boiling it, and now he had to take it to his horses.

Between the courtyard in front of the church and the convent yard just north there was a wide opening in the wall, barricaded about four feet high with bags of earth. Bourne scrambled over the barrier. He rapped his rifle barrel on the stonework and cursed. He stopped a moment in the dark to feel the front sight. It was undamaged.

Horses snorted softly in the convent yard. On beyond, in the stockaded cattle pen outside the walls, cattle were bawling with hunger. They were starving, Bourne thought wearily. The horses weren't having it much better, either.

"Who's down there?" a sentry on the outer wall challenged.

"Who do you think? It's me."

"Who the hell is *me*?"

"What's the difference? I came to feed my horses. Go back to sleep."

"I wish I could," the sentry said.

Bourne's *grulla*, Cactus, was already coming to the sound of his voice, blowing and pawing. Other hungry animals crowded in as Bourne fed Cactus from his hand. They followed him as he worked on into the yard to find the gray cavalry horse he had captured.

He gave the rest of the corn to the gray and then he stood beside it for a few moments, almost asleep on his feet. The sentry's voice roused him. "If you've got a horse, you're supposed to be over at headquarters right now."

"What for?" Bourne asked irritably.

"Courier service. What else would Travis want men with horses for?"

Bourne walked back through the yard with the hungry horses following all the way to the barricade. He went through the gate in the low plaza wall and on down to headquarters, in a room of the south barracks.

As he stepped inside a shell exploded in the plaza behind him. About twenty men were gathered in the room, their gaunt, unshaven faces shadowy in the candlelight. Captain Forsyth was there, his handsome features slack with weariness. Lieutenant Dickerson was sitting on the edge of a table, staring at the floor.

Colonel Travis was the only clean-shaved man present, the only one whose shirt didn't look like it had been walked on for a week. He said, "I think I've made our position clear enough, men, and so I'm going to call one more time for volunteers."

A cannon ball struck the outside wall. Dust drifted down through the candlelight and settled on the table, and Lieutenant Dickerson reached out slowly and began to trace some design in the film with his forefinger.

"We must maintain our lines of communication," Travis said.

"Seems like it's all one way, Colonel," a man said. "Messengers go out, but nothing comes back."

"Colonel Bonham returned, and now he's gone again."

"What good did it do?" someone asked.

"We've not been abandoned by Texas!" Travis said. "Our situation, I'll grant you, is urgent, and that's all the more reason we've got to keep couriers informing the people of Texas of affairs here. Relief may be coming even now—I'm sure that it is—"

103

"Then what do we need to send out more messengers for, Colonel?" Bourne asked.

"To speed the relieving columns!"

After several moments of silence Captain Forsyth said, "The Colonel asked for volunteers."

Men looked at each other. They stared at the floor. They studied Travis and the other officers. No one spoke.

Behind their silence was a stubborn desperation and a growing doubt that Texans were going to rally as strongly as Travis had suggested. And there was the memory of couriers who had gone out before, a lot of them, and only one had returned, with disappointing news.

Bourne tried to remember them. Dr. Sutherland and John Smith that first day, and two or three others about the same time. Bill Johnson had gone out on his fleet chestnut that first day, also, and that same night, Lance Smithers.

Captain Martin the next day. Bourne could remember that well enough. He and Martin were both from Gonzales, and if any place in Texas could be expected to send help, Gonzales was it. But no one had come. Ben Highsmith and Bob Brown had ridden away only two or three days after the siege began, carrying messages for help.

Hank Warnell just a few days ago. Then Colonel Bonham last night—or was it the night before? Besides all those messengers, several men who weren't in the army, had left Bexar after Dr. Sutherland and Smith scouted the Mexican cavalry and rode back with the news.

There was no doubt in Bourne's mind that Texas knew what was happening at the Alamo.

Other men seemed to be thinking along the same lines, for no one volunteered. They held a stubborn silence, while the Mexican artillery, those goddamned, unsleeping guns, kept pounding, pounding, pounding.

"Very well," Travis said, "if no one cares to volunteer, we'll draw straws to see who goes."

Dickerson stood up. He took a handful of corn from his pocket and marked one of the kernels with ink, blowing on it until it was dry. He dropped them into his hat and shook it.

One by one they drew. Bourne hesitated when he reached into the high-held hat and grasped a kernel. It squeezed out of his fingers. He took another and rolled it out on the table and it was unmarked, but on his forefinger there was a small smudge of ink.

104

Captain Juan Seguin, who had been sitting in a dark corner, came forward and drew the marked kernel. He smiled and shrugged. The others turned to leave.

"Wait a moment!" Travis said. "I'd like to impress on you how much I need Captain Seguin right here. We're short of officers and they're getting very little, or no, rest. I—"

"He drew the black bean, Colonel," someone said.

"Nevertheless, I need him more here than—"

"What the hell did we draw for then?" someone asked angrily.

"I don't mind, Colonel Travis," Seguin said quietly. "I accept the result. There is one thing, though, I will have to borrow someone's good horse, since mine—"

"I need you here!" Travis said.

There was a rebellious mutter in the room that even Travis could not quiet. Seguin raised his hand. "I will go."

Men were streaming out of the room. Bourne stepped forward and said, "I have two horses, Captain. You can have your choice."

"I thank you." Seguin made a little bow. "But first, I should like to ask Colonel Bowie if I may use his horse."

"There's a *grulla* with a blaze on his forehead—triangular, it is—and a gray Mexican cavalry horse."

"I know them," Seguin said. "And again I thank you, Daniel Bourne."

Juan Seguin went to see his good friend, Jim Bowie. Ham was sitting by the bed, nodding. Bowie had twisted his blankets into a tangle and was gripping them with both hands as he lay on his back staring at the ceiling.

Seguin straightened the blankets and drew them up over Bowie's chest. He saw no recognition in the sick man's eyes when he asked Bowie how he was.

"It is Juan Seguin, Diego. I have come to ask if I may use your horse."

Bowie's breathing was labored. He stared at Seguin and recognition grew slowly in his eyes. He nodded, and then he clutched the blankets again, twisting them with hands from which the tan was fading to a strange paleness.

Ham was awake then. He rearranged the blankets, saying, "Here now, Mistuh Jim, you got to keep them covers on you."

"Take good care of him," Seguin said. He went out knowing that he would never see Jim Bowie alive again.

Bourne was not asleep when Seguin came to him. He had

105

been sleeping as if drugged, but then shooting and wild yelling had erupted on the east side of the Alamo. Sentries began to fire and shout.

Weary men had risen, stumbling about as they grabbed their weapons and ran toward the walls. But it had been a false alarm, another diversion by the Mexican army to break the sleep of the tired defenders of the Alamo.

"My corporal wishes to use one of your horses," Seguin said. "And then, later, Colonel Travis will send another courier, who wishes to use your other horse."

Bourne rose and fumbled in the dark for the saddles. The silver-mounted one was over against the wall. He had rubbed it well and polished the silver trimmings. "If you go near Gonzales, would you ask George Tumlinson to keep this for me? Whoever uses the horse can get another saddle."

"I will do this," Seguin said.

A shadowy figure was waiting outside to help Seguin carry the gear.

"Go with God," Bourne told them both.

"Christ's sake, will you stop that infernal jabbering and let us get some sleep!" someone on the floor said angrily.

Once more Bourne lay down. He was just drifting off when the Mexicans broke out with a new clamor, this time outside the north wall of the plaza. Once more he and others in the barracks jumped up and seized their weapons. They never knew when an attack was real, or just a fiendish stratagem to drive them closer to exhaustion.

With the hoofs of the horses muffled with sacking, Captain Seguin and Corporal Antonio Arocha slipped from the Alamo quietly. When they were a few hundred feet from the walls, they turned north, still leading their horses.

Now and then they stopped to listen, to crouch low and peer along the ground for signs of a dug-in outpost. They mounted and walked their horses slowly north. Off to the left they heard stealthy forms creeping in toward the Alamo, and it was not long after that when the wild noise of the fake attack against the north wall began.

Covered somewhat by the sounds, Seguin and Arocha quickly removed the sacking from the feet of their horses and turned east, still holding their slow pace. It was not a dark night out here on the plain. Far ahead they saw a wooded area, the dark bulk of it looming in soft outlines.

106

They were close to it when the stamp of a hoof directly ahead gave the first warning. An instant later they saw the cavalry patrol.

Arocha groaned softly. It seemed that they had been almost free. His fears had been leaving him and he had been feeling the handsome mountings of the saddle and admiring the strength and grace of the horse under him, and now—trapped!

"Do not run until I do," Seguin said softly. "Then, to the woods."

A voice challenged them. "Who goes?"

"My brother and I," Seguin called in the same language of the officer. "We go to see about our cows that have run away."

He sensed the lessening of tension in the patrol. He gambled his life on that feeling.

"Approach!" the officer commanded.

"We are coming."

Still without haste, straight toward the cavalry, Seguin and Arocha rode. Seguin saw a man swing down to check his cinch. He saw another man returning his pistol to the scabbard.

The two couriers were only forty feet away when Seguin jabbed his spurs into his horse and swung to the right. Arocha, who had been waiting for that move until his heart was nearly bursting, was but a split second behind his leader.

Bent low over their saddles, they rode for their lives. The officer shouted. Pistols flared in the night, fired hastily by men caught by surprise. The couriers made it to the woods, and from there Seguin knew a way that took them swiftly on, while the patrol became entangled.

Only three of them were close when Seguin and Arocha burst from the woods, and those two fell steadily behind as the couriers rode with a solid knowledge of what lay ahead of each jump of their horses.

After a time the pursuers gave up. Seguin and Arocha were on their way to Goliad with a message for Colonel Fannin.

Shortly after the couriers left the fort, Davy Crockett went over the barricade and disappeared like smoke into the night. He checked the outpost sentry beyond the *acequia,* startling the man as he ghosted out of the dark.

"I'm going on out a piece. I'll whistle soft, like a bird, when I come back."

"There might be some of that last bunch still sneaking around out there," the sentry said.

107

"Good! Just be sure *they* shoot me, not you." Crockett chuckled softly and slipped away. He went on until he was well away from the fort, and then he stood still.

During a lull in the artillery fire he heard the distant pistol shots. One, two, three, four—and then a battery fired and wrecked the momentary quiet. He listened for a few more minutes before trotting back to the fort.

Travis had fallen asleep at the table in headquarters. He groaned and shook his head when Crockett woke him and told him about the pistol shots in the direction the couriers had gone.

Admitting a brutal fact that he would not have allowed before the men, Travis said, "We don't know what happens to our couriers, Colonel Crockett. The truth is that we're sure about only one of them—Bonham, the first time he left."

"Garza is ready to leave." Alexandro de la Garza had volunteered for courier duty after he found out that no one else would volunteer.

Travis took a paper from the table, a copy of the message Seguin had carried. "Send him out, Colonel Crockett."

Garza led Bourne's *grulla* up to the gate. Small and tough and unafraid was the Mexican—and a daring rider. He smiled quickly at Crockett and shook his hand. He said to Lieutenant Dickerson, "I could take your baby, your Angelina?"

Dickerson shook his head.

"I will get there, Lieutenant. I have no fear that I will not. If you wish your Angelina to be safe—"

"Just get the message through."

Garza led the horse out. One more courier disappearing into the darkness, a darkness that was on the Alamo even in daylight because no man knew what happened to a courier after he left.

It seemed that Texas had forgotten the Alamo.

"Just one message telling us that help was on the way would be worth one hundred reinforcements actually here," Dickerson said.

The effective force in the Alamo was now 152 men, tired men who ate cornbread and tough beef, who manned their posts without orders, who killed every Mexican soldier who exposed himself within rifle range in daytime.

Who looked eastward for help that did not come.

CHAPTER 14

"You're going to fool with that thing until you blow your head off," said Billy Wells, watching Hawkins tinkering with a Mexican musket. They were on the roof of the west barracks, their assigned post. "How'd you make that fuse?"

"First, you know everything, and then you're asking questions. How did I make the fuse? By the use of my remarkable, inventive brain, that's how. 'Tis something I would recommend to all Georgians, if they had a brain to use."

"How *did* you make it, Mark?"

"I biled a bit of cow hoof, and a fine stew it made. Then I dipped my string into it and then into some of this fine, dirty Mexican powder."

Wells looked north as two batteries fired. "Will it work?"

"That is what I'm just before finding out." Hawkins poured a pinch of powder on the roof, laid one end of the fuse in it, and began to strike steel against flint. The tiny cone of loose powder caught. The fuse began to burn, sputtering and smoking, and then, half way its length, it fizzed out.

Wells laughed. "Fine fuse. Phew! It's the stinkingest fuse I ever smelled!"

Hawkins shook his head sadly at the smelly mess. "That no-good Mexican powder is the fault of it."

McGregor was lying on his belly with his chin on his arms. "Why didn't you use good powder from your own horn? A pinch would have been enough."

Hawkins gave a long sigh. "Now why didn't I indeed!"

"High one!" someone yelled.

The ball from the ditch battery truly was a high one, as if the gunners had dug the trail of the piece in and tried to stand the cannon on end. Clear over the church the shot carried, and blew up somewhere outside the fort. Men cheered and laughed.

"Too bad it is that it didn't carry down to their south battery that's been pecking at the gate, and blow the lot of them to smithereens," McGregor said.

Three more times the water battery tried high-arcing shots and they all were long. "They're trying to lob a few through

109

the open top of the church, that's what," Hawkins said. "They've no respect for churches, those bandits." He resumed his study of the long bomb problem.

On the north end of the same barracks, Charles Clark, a dark-faced Missourian, waited patiently for the next round from the ditch battery. Each time it had fired an officer had popped his head up for a quick look, and then ducked back before he drew a rifle shot.

Clark's cheek was flat against the stock of a Pennsylvania rifle his father had used before him. His deep-set eyes were dark with concentration. He guessed it would be on the right side of the earthworks shielding the cannon. That officer fancied himself as being smart. He'd kept shifting from one place to another.

Clark saw the puff of smoke from the battery. He took a deep breath and held it. His guess was right. He touched the hair trigger and even as the rifle made its short, flat bark he knew he was dead on the mark.

"You got him!" Joe Kerr said. "I was set for him on the other side. How many does that make today?"

Clark was reloading. "Just one." He grinned. "Of course that's the only shot I've taken."

That was the last time the ditch battery tried to be a howitzer. It went back to throwing solid rounds against the north wall.

That north wall was being shaken, Major Jameson observed as he made his rounds of the fort. The Mexican artillery was concentrating on the northeast end of it. By Jeems, it was a good thing they didn't have regular siege guns, or there wouldn't be a wall standing anywhere around the plaza by now.

He ordered work parties to throw dirt against the bottom of the wall and to add more dirt to the breastworks south of the wall.

Like everyone else in the Alamo, he knew the only way the fort would be taken was by a determined rush of infantry. They could hammer with their batteries until Kingdom Come and knock all sorts of holes in the walls, but if they wanted the Alamo, they would have to come and take it, hand to hand.

It was that thought that prompted Jameson to go up the ladder to the east wall. His heart jumped. Riders were coming toward the fort. And then he saw the whip of a pennon and knew that it was a Mexican patrol coming in from some night ride.

The reaction hit him hard. All the worries and the sleepless nights seemed to weigh on him in one hard-descending moment.

Goddamn! What was the sense of being here when the rest of Texas didn't care?

The plaza seemed to have grown longer as he walked the length of it to see Jim Bowie. Dr. Mitchasson was just coming out. He squinted in the sun and the lines that had deepened above his beard were cruelly shown. He looked as if he hadn't slept for a solid week.

"How is he?" Jameson asked.

"He's holding better than I thought, while the disease runs its course. Both Pollard and I think it's typhoid-pneumonia. If he gets over it, he'll be a long, long time recovering." Mitchasson hurried away toward the hospital.

Jameson paused at the doorway. It sounded like a new battery to the south. He listened for a moment. Well, what was the difference? They were everywhere now.

He went in to see Jim Bowie.

The sick man was having a lucid interval. "Benito!" he said, and smiled. "How are you?"

"How are *you* is the problem, Jim."

"Weak as a sick cat, but I feel better today."

"Good!" Jameson smiled, but inside him was a heavy fear. Jim Bowie's todays were those moments when his head was clear, and all the rest was tortured nights of fever and restlessness.

"How does it go, Benito?"

"Fine. We haven't lost a man. The walls are all holding well, and we expect help any moment."

Bowie watched him steadily. "You never were easy with a lie, were you? Do you really expect help?"

They looked at each other soberly. "We hope for it," Jameson said. "That isn't too much to ask, is it?"

"Hope. . . ." Bowie drifted off somewhere into the whirling, flashing world of fever. "No!" he said. "No we won't!" And what he meant had no meaning to Major Jameson, who took a long look at him and turned away.

Travis' servant ran up to him when he was a few feet from the doorway. "Looky here, Major, what Colonel Travis give to me!" Joe was holding a flintlock pistol with a thumb-sized bore.

"Do you know how to handle that thing, Joe?"

"I surely do, I surely do. I'm going to shoot me a lot of Mexicans with this, Colonel Jameson. I surely am!"

Jameson went up on the south barracks. Yes, it was a newly seated battery, and it seemed to be dedicated to keeping the gunners away from the eighteen-pounder. They had run their piece down the ramp, but the Mexican gun kept popping shells at the platform where they had been a short time before.

Jake Walker was gathering scrap for the guns in the chapel. From the cooks, who were making jerky, he got a cast iron kettle. He broke it into scraps and put them in his leather bucket. From the armory he was given four defective pistols. He knocked everything off them that would fit into a twelve-pound bore.

His greatest haul was a pile of rusted nails that he found mixed with fragments of a rotted leather bag in a storeroom. The excavations to strengthen the walls was always a good source. There he found some copper buttons and a rusted piece of Spanish breastplate armor that broke easily into sharp fragments.

He found a gold coin too, and that he put into his pocket after scraping some of the dirt away with a knife.

All around the plaza he picked up pieces of bombshells, until his leather bucket was heavily loaded. He was going back to the church when he spied the edge of metal sticking from the ground not far from the doorway. He pried it out and broke the dirt away.

It was a silver crucifix, about eight inches high, wide and heavy. It might be a hundred years old, he thought, holding it up and turning it in his hand.

Mrs. Dickerson and a group of Mexican women holding children watched him from the doorway of the chapel. They looked at each other in horror as Walker suddenly bent the cross in his hands and dropped it into his bucket.

One of them with Indian strain strong across her wide features nodded her head in agreement with Walker's act. She said, "The padres of old in this mission often thought that Christ spoke best from the mouths of cannons and the rifles of soldiers. Now let the crucifix speak back to the soldiers."

Excitement leaped suddenly along the north wall as Walker stolidly carried his bucket of scrap into the chapel.

"The hell it ain't!" Billy Wells said, pointing with his rifle. "See that white plume on his hat, and all those fancy officers around him? That's the high cockalorum hisself, old Santa Anna!"

McGregor squinted. "You may be right, lad."

Wells and Wilson ran to the north end of the roof. There were others there ahead of them, with the same intentions that they had, and, among the very first, Charles Clark.

The group of officers was a fair piece away, a mighty long carry for Clark's rifle. He knelt and rested the piece on a canvas sheet someone had thrown over the rock coping to keep fragments from flying viciously when struck by cannon shots. The target was facing him head-on, motionless. Clark sighted several feet above the white plume.

The water battery fired, and at the same time the corner eight-pounder on Clark's right made its shuddering boom. Clark's nerves jumped. He let his breath out and cursed under his breath.

Two or three riflemen tried their luck. One of the horses near Santa Anna jumped and jostled another horse, and then the whole group moved a little. They rode on to the right. Clark's front sight followed above the white plume. He could get the horse, he was sure.

But that was a wicked compromise. It was like lung-shooting a deer because you were afraid you might miss its head. It was the man—or nothing.

Again the little cavalcade stopped. One of the eight-pounders rocked out, but this time it didn't bother Clark. He touched the trigger, and during that same tick of time he saw the target knee his horse to the left and point at something.

And then Santa Anna and his staff moved away briskly on their tour of inspection, angling northeast, farther and farther out of hopeful range. Riflemen on the north end of the east wall tried, but the distance was much too great.

"Crockett should have been here!" Wells said regretfully.

"You look like a young coyote that just saw a rabbit dive into a hole after he had one taste of fur," Wilson said.

"That's presactly what I feel like too."

For a full two minutes Clark remained kneeling, with his head bowed, running his hand over the beautiful maple inlet work on the stock of his rifle.

"What's the matter, Clark?" Wilson asked. "You feel like that hungry coyote too?"

113

"Those cannons! Those miserable cannons of ours haven't hit one single thing, not one single thing they ever shot at!" Clark rose and stalked back down to his regular position.

That afternoon the gunners of the twelve-pounder midway of the west wall, having watched with extreme interest for some time the couriers coming like the spokes of a wheel to a hub, which happened to be a house on the east back of the San Antonio, decided to see if they could crack the hub.

Lieutenant Evans laid the sights.

Patrick Henry Herndon touched the powder train with his torch. "Fire in the hole!"

Old Bolivar, the name they had given the piece, belched and bucked back against the trail. The ball was dead in line, but short.

The next shot was there. Dust flew from Santa Anna's headquarters and men came rushing out. The gun crew and those along the west wall cheered lustily.

It was only a passing triumph. There wasn't enough powder left to use on a distant target, which would be quickly abandoned anyway if the firing continued.

"There noo, lad," McGregor told Clark, "you see our cannons are of some use after all."

"They punched a hole in the wall—and quit. They didn't get Santa Anna." For the fleeting time left to him, Clark would never cease wondering what might have been if he had not let those two cannon shots in the morning make him jump out of his skin like a scared old woman.

Charles Clark would never know, but for one fraction of a second he had held within his grasp the saving of the Alamo.

It was then the eighth day of the siege, March 1, 1836.

CHAPTER 15

THROUGH THE DARK OVERCAST of a cold night, John Smith led the group of fighters coming to the relief of the Alamo. They were very close, and the fact sharpened all of Smith's senses, for this last mile would be the most dangerous distance of the whole trip.

"Hold up, Al," he said to Captain Martin, leader of the force. "I've got to scout ahead." He knew exactly where he was in relation to the fort, but he also knew from the messages that Travis had sent during the last week that the Mexican army had encircled the Alamo with an ever-tightening grip.

He dismounted and walked ahead slowly, watching the flashes as the besieging batteries fired. There seemed to be a hole straight ahead, that was, as far as the artillery was concerned.

His greatest worry was that a roving patrol of cavalry would bump against the reinforcements, and then, before swarms of Mexicans came running to the noise, Martin would have to take his men hell for leather to the fort.

That part was the worst of all his fears. Those in the Alamo would cut loose and riddle the very hell out of their own reinforcements.

Smith walked on, feeling out the night.

Behind him the reinforcements waited quietly, thirty-two of them, the men of Gonzales rallied by Captain Martin, their friend and neighbor. They were married men, men with children. They knew what they were getting into, but they had come. They had a stake in Texas—and were willing to fight for it.

They had comrades in the Alamo, and they came for that reason too.

It was in Gonzales that the Mexican government had decided in the fall of 1835 to take back a brass cannon that had been loaned to the town. Colonel Domingo Ugartechea sent his men to seize it. They were greeted by a banner which read: *Come And Take It*, and behind the banner were armed *tejanos*.

Colonel Ugartechea's men made a determined effort but they didn't get the cannon. Many of those men who kept their cannon were on the plain this night, listening to the darkness, waiting for Smith to come back.

Their only fault lay in being so few in number.

"Those cannons make me nervous," Bill Dearduff said.

"You'll get used to them before this little sashay is over," someone commented.

"Quiet!" Lieutenant Bob White said. "I think he's coming back."

Smith came softly out of the darkness. "I think it's clear— for a ways."

Once more the men of Gonzales went forward. Out of nowhere the rider seemed to appear. One moment there was nothing and then he was there, sitting his dark horse a little to the right and ahead of the group.

A dozen men had pistols half drawn when the voice said coolly, "You men want to get into the fort, of course. You're heading straight for a regiment of sappers." He turned his horse. "Follow me."

There was a Louisiana drawl in his speech. He turned his back to them, waiting for a moment, and then he started off slowly. They followed him.

Someone let out a sigh. "I'm glad we met someone who knows how to sneak in."

"Who is that fellow?"

"One of the Louisiana volunteers, I guess."

John Smith had been relieved too, but the feeling did not last long. The rider, whoever he was, and no matter how un-accented his use of English, was leading them west. Maybe I'm mixed up, Smith thought. Maybe I've lost my own sense of direction for a minute.

He kept following the pilot. No, by God, he wasn't off in his own directions! The man was taking them west, straight toward Bexar. Smith leaned over and whispered to Martin, "I'm after thinking we'd best shoot that bastard. He's going——"

The guide's horse grunted as the man hit him with his spurs. He surged away into the darkness, bent low.

"No shooting!" Martin said urgently.

Smith said bitterly, "I should have ridden up beside him and clubbed him down." He wasted no more time in vain regrets, but turned once more southwest. And now it was more urgent than ever to make haste, but it must be done slowly.

One-Eye Guerrero crouched at his outpost east of the church. He scorned the pit that sentries had dug, for such a thing made a hump in the night, and in a pit, feeling falsely secure, one might go to sleep and never waken.

He heard the sound of *zapadores*, the scraping of shovels. They were closer. Always they were closer. And then he heard the footsteps. He put his ear quickly to the earth.

The cursed cannons fired.

Guerrero cocked his rifle, holding back the trigger so that it was done silently. He looked close to the ground. There were more steps. He saw movement, but he knew that shadows moved when the eyes strained hard, and he was not one to fire at shadows.

The curse of the devil himself on those cannons that were never still!

116

Some moments later he knew. Yes, it was movement. Yes, it was a man. He levelled his rifle. The orders were very strong: fire only when you knew beyond doubt that it was not a courier. But messengers were supposed to be on horses, not treading softly on foot.

By the pinch of cotton stuck to his front sight Guerrero aimed. The man kept coming and now he was as good as dead. Only the order, which was slipping fast from Guerrero's mind, kept him from firing. In another second. . . .

"Texas sentry?" the dark figure said, stopping.

The English words were in Guerrero's head, but they came out Spanish when he spoke. "Who comes?"

The man hesitated, and it was then that Guerrero almost pulled the trigger.

"John Smith!"

Guerrero let the hammer down. No Mexican in the world could say that name as this one had. "I almost shot you, Juan."

Smith ran forward. Now that he was safe, and for quicker understanding, he spoke in Spanish. "Run to the fort and make sure the sentries are told not to shoot. I have men coming in soon."

"That is truly good news."

"Run!" Smith turned and raced back to where he had left the men from Gonzales.

"Is it clear?" Martin asked. "There's cavalry coming."

Because of his running Smith had not heard the sounds, but now he did. That sonofabitch who had tried to mislead them! Not too fast, but they were coming, and it sounded like an almighty plenty of them. "We've still got to move in slow," he said.

Lieutenant Kimbell spoke coolly. "If we get into a night scrape out here, we'll be scattered from hell to breakfast in no time. Let's make a run—"

"No!" Smith said sharply. "If we do that, we'll likely take a working-over from the fort that'll be worse than any cavalry can give us. We've got to move slow until we know for sure that the sentries have been warned about us."

When the back walls of the Alamo loomed in the dark, they could hear someone shouting, "Don't fire! Texas men coming! Don't fire, boys!"

"Let's go!" Smith yelled.

In spite of the warning, a sentry whose mind was groggy from lack of rest fired and struck Jon Lindley in the foot.

The men of Gonzales rushed into the fort moments later, and before long the defenders came running to greet them, shouting, laughing.

Relief that they had given up was here! There were Texas men who had not forgotten them after all!

Old friends shook each other's hand, and as the garrison mingled with the new arrivals, men coming to the scene got the impression that a whole army had arrived.

That was Colonel Travis' first impression, until Captain Martin reported to him at headquarters.

"Only thirty-two?" Travis tried to hide his disappointment.

"You won't find thirty-two better men in Texas—or anywhere else, Colonel," Martin said hotly. He was a little tired himself.

"I don't doubt that." Travis sat down. "That wasn't what I was thinking, Captain. I was hoping. . . ." Travis rubbed his hand across his eyes, and then he stared for a moment at the wall.

In the light of three candles on the table Martin had a clear look at Travis' face. It was a shock. It was impossible that a man could have aged like that in one week! Travis was a haggard old man, his eyes sunken, bloodshot, desperate.

Martin was sorry then that he had spoken irritably, for he realized how Travis must have hoped and prayed for help. His spirits must have soared when he heard that reinforcements were just outside the Alamo—and then he had found out that there were only thirty-two.

"How many men have you lost?" Martin asked.

"None!" Travis rose and some of the weariness seemed to leave him. He straightened his shoulders. "We've inflicted heavy losses on the enemy. We've held this place and delayed that whole army, Captain, and with God's help, we'll stave them off until there's a Texas army here big enough to go out and meet them in open battle!"

Martin nodded. He could see that Travis actually believed what he was saying.

"It's been a nerve-wracking wait, but we knew it would take a little time for men to get organized. You're the first, Captain. From now on we can expect heavy reinforcements."

Martin was on the verge of crushing that hope, but he listened to the happy shouts outside and he looked at the hard fighting spirit in Travis' eyes, and he thought, Smith will tell him what we know.

118

John Smith came in then, and with him a rush of officers who were talking excitedly. They all looked as worn and drawn as their commander but for the moment they were cheered by the arrival of the Gonzales men.

Martin went out to confer with Lieutenant Kimbell about quarters for the company. The men were already making their own arrangements.

There was no lack of space in the Alamo, Martin thought. He walked out into the plaza, stumbling through small pits made by bombshells. The artillery was firing steadily. No wonder the defenders looked ready to drop and fall asleep.

Martin stood quietly, looking at the long run of the western wall. As Colonel Neill had said often, one thousand men would be fair garrison strength for this place.

According to Travis, the effective force was now 185, including the wounded Jon Lindley.

Martin walked toward the hospital to see how Jon was.

It was about 3:30 in the morning of the night of March 1, 1836.

CHAPTER 16

CAPTAIN WILLIAM CAREY, a Virginian, in charge of the eight-pound batteries at the north wall of the fort, had slept uneasily for three hours of the night, but even in his rest the pounding of one battery kept running through his being.

At dawn he went to the north wall to see if he had been dreaming. He had not. The ditch battery was no longer firing from its old position. It was now within pistol range of the north wall, dug in behind a thick embankment of brown earth, with curving breastworks for musket men on both wings, and with trenches angling back to another strong emplacement, which undoubtedly was heavily manned with reinforcements who could rush down the angling trench to support the men defending the advanced gun.

It took Carey only a few moments of observation to know that the battery held a terrible threat to the Alamo.

He watched it fire.

Through a narrow embrasure in the earthworks the muzzle appeared suddenly. The piece belched a solid round against

the wall, already showing the effects of persistent cannonading.

Three riflemen had fired during the time when the muzzle
was looking at them. Now it was gone. Carey squinted at the
embrasure. The cannon, of course, had been run back down
a ramp for reloading, he knew, but why couldn't rifle fire
knock the gunners over?

"Where's Clark?" he asked.

"He given up on it, Captain," a man said. He was reloading his rifle. "So am I. Somebody's got to show his haid afore
I'm wasting any more powder. I been bouncin' shots offn that
barrel in hopes of catching a man at one side or tother, but iffn
I did, it ain't slowed 'em down none."

"Go get Travis."

"Jest as soon as I load this here rifle gun, Cap'n. I been
thinking I'll git old Davy hisself, too, but I don't reckon even
him is going to do no good."

After the man left, Carey saw something that his tired eyes
had missed before. After each shot, when the muzzle kicked
back, the embrasure was quickly blocked by men lying behind
the embankment. Then, probably just as fire was applied to
the touch-hole, with the piece run back up the ramp, the
blocking was pulled aside.

Sighting was no problem; they had the whole north wall
as a target.

Travis and Crockett arrived soon with the messenger Carey
had sent.

"That'll never do," Travis said, after only a moment. "Can't
you knock that out with your eight-pounders, Captain?"

Carey shook his head. "I doubt it."

"Try it!"

The gunners were digging, throwing dirt against the wall to
bolster it. "All right men," Carey said, "you'll have to aim
and fire your guns like rifles."

They had seen the battery and they knew what he meant.
Carey tried to time each shot to strike when the embrasure
was cleared. The first ball sponged into the earth embankment with a harmless plop.

"Fire in the touch-hole!"

The second shot was low. It blew dirt toward the dark muzzle of the Mexican cannon, but an instant later the piece
hurled another ball against the wall. The third shot was off to
the left.

120

Smoothbore brass cannons and rusty balls were not quite good enough for the kind of accuracy needed to silence that dangerous battery with a mere three shots.

"We can get it in time," Carey said.

Travis shook his head. "We haven't got the powder to spare."

Crockett had been studying the problem. "We can go out there and take it."

Travis glanced right and left at the supporting batteries, at the entrenchments. Some canny Mexican commander was hoping that men would try to rush that advanced battery.

It could be done but it would cost too much.

"You know what they're covering that hole with, water-soaked planks," Crockett said. "They swaller a rifle ball like an old bull 'gator shot in the tail."

The other riflemen were looking at Davy Crockett and waiting. They expected some miracle from him and old Betsy, some kind of shot that no one in the world but he could make.

But there was no way for a rifle to do any more than annoy the men behind the Mexican battery.

Crockett sensed the feeling around him. "Like the fellow said when he went to his wedding and found out the girl had changed her mind, 'I got to have something out of my trip over the mountain.' So he kissed the girl's mother and got back on his mule."

Crockett raised Betsy casually and put a rifle ball down the mouth of the cannon. They all knew that it did no harm, but Crockett was a man who wouldn't disappoint an audience. He left them laughing.

On the roof of the west barracks, Billy Wells watched Crockett striding down the plaza, and said, "I wisht I'd heard what he told that bunch. I could stand a little chirking up."

"You mean you've forgotten about the Gonzales men so quick?" Wilson asked.

"No, by God, I haven't! That's one thing that's happened around here to make a man feel better. We didn't maybe know what we was getting into when we come trotting into here, but those Gonzales boys, they knew—and they came anyway."

His spirits cheered, Wells went up the roof to see how Hawkins was doing with his long bombs.

121

"You're just in time, me lad," said Hawkins. "I've got this lovely thing fused. Now if you'll kindly leap over the wall and stand there for a moment, I'll light me little invention and drop it down beside you."

"You—! Aw, hell," Wells said, grinning.

"You mean to stand there with whiskers on your chin like peach fuzz and say you've no interest in testing the wondrous workings of me invention?"

"No, by Jeems! Wait till we get a few soldiers down there."

"That's me firm and devoted intention," Hawkins said.

McGregor was looking toward Bexar. "We have more visitors."

Zapadores battalions of Toluca and Aldama were marching into Bexar, with flags flying. Bands in the old military plaza struck up to greet them.

Those on the barracks roof didn't know who the new arrivals were, and wouldn't have cared a damn for the names of the units if they had known. All they knew was that they were seeing more Mexican reinforcements, more hundreds added to the encircling pressure.

Suddenly the laughter was gone.

"Just about now," Wilson said, "we're like an old boar coon on a real high stump, with forty-seven dogs around him." Unconsciously, he turned to look east.

The sunken road out there was swarming with the Mexicans who had moved in on it the day before.

Hawkins said, "All that old boar coon of yours has got to do is tear the throat out of every dog that tries to jump up on the stump. There'll be a bunch of them biting dirt before they finally get him."

It was the first time any of that group had admitted aloud that they were between a rock and a hard place, with every hour dimming their chances.

For a while at least the banter was no good. They went back to their individual posts, and most of them fell asleep, with their nerves twitching as the cannonade went on and on.

The morning was almost gone when rifles began to crackle along the north wall. Wells and his companions roused up, guilty, startled, looking first toward the plain to the west before they realized that the excitement was north of them.

Someone on the north defense waved his hat and gave a quavering cattle yell. "Ride, you bastard, ride!"

"It's Bonham!"

Wells and the others ran to the north end of the barracks. The man was on a light dun. A white handkerchief was tied to his hat. Bonham, sure enough!

A cavalry patrol was on his tail and another was trying to intercept him from the east. It quickened Wells' heart just to see the way he rode, as beautiful a rider as Wells had ever seen astride a horse.

He was coming down from the northeast, between the old mill where a battery was seated and the heavy concentration of troops along the Gonzales road.

Zapadores dropped their shovels and grabbed up muskets to fire at him. The cavalry behind him took shots. Bonham waved his hat at the cheering men on the walls of the Alamo. They turned the cavalry patrols back with rifle fire.

For the second time during the siege, Colonel Bonham came through the gates untouched.

His daring ride, and a hope for good news from him, raised the spirits of the defenders. But the drop back toward despair was all the harder when the word was passed that Bonham had no good news. Travis made no official announcement of what message Bonham brought, but the text of it filtered through the ranks nonetheless.

No aid for the Alamo.

A convention was to be held at Washington-on-the-Brazos, a meeting of dignified representatives to determine the future of Texas.

When that news passed, it was received with curses. The Alamo didn't need a convention to determine its future; it was being strangled to death for want of more Texans like the men of Gonzales.

From Colonel Bonham, his boyhood friend, Travis received nothing but confirmation of the brutal facts that John Smith had already brought. The Alamo was on its own. Fear of Santa Anna was already driving colonists away from the results of ten years or more of sweat and blood, their homes and futures.

To the president of the convention at Washington-on-the-Brazos, Travis wrote:

". . . *I have so fortified the place that the walls are generally proof against cannon balls, and I still continue to entrench on the inside, and strengthen the walls by throwing up earth . . . we have been so fortunate as to not lose a*
123

man from any cause, and we have killed many of the enemy. *The spirits of the men are still high, although they have had much to depress them....*

"*Colonel Fannin is said to be on the march to this place with re-inforcements; but I fear it is not true, as I have repeatedly sent to him for aid without receiving any . . . I will, however, do the best I can under the circumstances; and I feel confident that the determined spirit and desperate courage heretofore evinced by my men will not fail them in the last struggle; and although they may be sacrificed to the vengeance of a Gothic enemy, the victory will cost the enemy so dear that it will be worse than a defeat....*

"*I hope your honorable body will hasten on re-inforcements, ammunition and provisions to our aid as soon as possible . . . if these things are promptly sent, and large reinforcements are hastened to this frontier, this neighborhood will be the great decisive battleground. The power of Santa Anna is to be met here or in the colonies. We had better meet it here than to suffer a war of desolation to rage in our settlements.*

"*A blood-red banner waves from the church at Bexar, and in the camp above us, in token that the war is one of vengeance against rebels. They have declared us such, and demanded that we should surrender at discretion, or this garrison should be put to the sword. Their threats have had no influence on me or my men, but to make all fight with desperation, and with that high-souled courage which characterizes the patriot who is willing to die in defense of his country's liberty and his own honor....*

"*The bearer of this will give your honorable body a statement more in detail, should he escape through the enemy's lines.*"

God and Texas! Victory or death!

To friends he wrote other letters. And several men of the garrison, who knew that John Smith was going to make another attempt to go out that night, stared at paper, benumbed by near exhaustion, and then they wrote for the last time to friends and loved ones.

"*. . . if I don't see you soon take kare of the Babies . . .*"

124

"I take pen in hand to say all is well with me and Bill, we have ben in a fite with Sesmas soldiers for morr than 1 week...."

"Dear Wife, it may be that i won't be home but we stil expet Fanning ... our Speerts are Good ... we have corn and beef in plenty ... i hit the front site on pas rifle to the left but we fixed it fine againe...."

In Bexar, where every thought of Santa Anna was known, or thought to be known, by the citizens, there was talk that on the morrow the citadel of the Alamo would be stormed.

This greatly worried Veedor Bustamente, who called Bernal to him and told him what to do.

The boy twisted and looked afraid. "But it is not as it was before. Now the soldiers are everywhere."

Veedor scowled. "It said that a large number of *tejanos* came into the fort last night. One small boy surely can go there," he said bitingly. "In my time, even though Comanches were all around, I—".

"Yes, Grandfather. I will go."

Another ancient of the town, Señora Carabajal, whose ears were bad, so that she had been little troubled by the ceaseless cannon fire, went for the first time in weeks to the church of San Fernando, not because she was particularly devout but because her daughter had kept her ten children in the house for so long that Señora Carabajal was greatly in need of a place to sit quietly for a time, with no little ones pawing at her old body and demanding attention.

She knelt with difficulty and said a few prayers and then she sat on the bench, sighing, happy with the peace of the cathedral.

It was then that the battery on top of the church fired.

Señora Carabajal could hear that sound, for the building trembled and dust flew through the air and the statue of the Virgin swayed a little before her eyes.

She cried aloud the names of Saints, and fled, screaming that the North Americans had destroyed the church, and when she was back in the house of her daughter, where the children seemed much better behaved than before, she could not be persuaded to believe other than that the North Americans truly had destroyed the church.

125

Nor would she go to see that it was not so; a woman of strong convictions was Señora Carabajal.

About that same time, Señora Ramon Musquiz, wife of the political *jefe* of Bexar, had been granted audience with his Excellency, Presidente of Mexico, Santa Anna.

She begged for the lives of the women trapped with their men in the Alamo.

"There is no need for you to be here," Santa Anna said. "It is well known that the glorious Army of Mexico, led by your Presidente, does not make war on women." He smiled. "Now, who is it that you have come to see about?"

"Señora Dickerson. She is the wife of a North American officer of the fort, your Excellency, with a child who does not yet have two years."

"She is North American too?"

Señora Musquiz swallowed. "Yes."

Santa Anna dispensed mercy with a careless flip of his hand. "They will be spared."

An aide was writing a note to that effect. It was sometimes difficult to see that all the little things which his Excellency wanted done were actually done; but it would be far more difficult for the aide if they were not done.

It was a rather chilly day, March 3, 1836.

CHAPTER 17

Now IT WAS the evening of March 3.

"What this here big doings all about?" Billy Wells asked Sergeant Hersee, who was passing the word on the west wall to all who could be spared from duty that they were to assemble in the church at once.

"If I knew, I would explain it to you," Hersee said, "and then you could stay here and go back to sleep."

"Just call a man a sergeant and he swells up like a poisoned pup," Wells grumbled. "Besides, I wasn't asleep!" he called after Hersee, who was going briskly on with his message.

They were coming from all parts of the Alamo, ragged, dirty men, bearded, their eyes hollowed by lack of rest.

"They're carrying Bowie out," Wilson said. "Look there."

One man at each corner of his cot, they were bringing Jim

126

Bowie to the meeting too. Men stood aside and looked down at him curiously as his bearers took him through the gate in the low wall.

Not since they entered the Alamo had so many men assembled in one place. They looked up at the evening sky above the church. Some of the sentries left on duty on the firing platforms were looking down, their figures sharply drawn against the fading light.

Darkness was already crouched in the corners of the ancient chapel. The women and children who stayed here in the strongest part of the fort had gone to a room off the sacristy.

Men cleared their throats. They shuffled around a little. Here and there one leaned on a rifle, dozing, for they had learned the hard lesson of all fighting men: any rest you can get, if only for a moment, must be taken when the chance is there.

Travis came in the wide front doorway, his uniform stained and rumpled, but still he cut a dashing figure as he walked through the waiting men and went up a short distance on the cannon ramp in the apse.

He stood with head bowed for a moment or two, and then he swept his gaze across the faces of the men of the Alamo and began to speak, so quietly at first that those near the doorway had to strain to hear his words.

"Men of Texas, in this brief respite from vigilance, I have called you here to speak of matters that every patriot must feel within his soul as deeply as I. The enemy is all about us. By day and night you have seen his stealthy encroachment upon this place." The power of Travis' voice was reaching now, strong and resonant.

"We have repulsed the Gothic forces of the enemy in every attempt he has made against our position, and we have spurned his offer to surrender and be destroyed by the sword."

With all his lawyer's skill he gave his men full credit for an heroic defense "of the outer walls of freedom, a defense that history will respect for all time."

His voice rose and fell with calculated intent.

"My couriers have brought me word that Colonel Fannin cannot march to the relief of this fort."

They took that in dead silence; the fact was already known to them.

"Therefore, it becomes doubly imperative that we defend to the last resources of our mortal strength this bastion of freedom, since it stands squarely across the ruthless path of a

127

determined and brutal invader, who, if he be turned back here, will be unable to ravage and pillage in the colonies."

He explained that the convention even then meeting in Washington-on-the-Brazos would undoubtedly declare for war.

A Tennessean murmured to his companion, "Hell, we done got one right here now."

"I say to you that we can expect at any moment a determined rush by the hordes encamped around us, and when that time comes, I call upon you for the supreme effort, as patriots, as defenders of the freedom you have preserved thus far, to sell your lives dearly, to slay them as they come upon you."

Hawkins muttered to McGregor, "I've the very same idea."

"Slay them as they charge our walls! Kill them as they come by esplanade! Kill them as they set foot upon these roofs! Kill them in the name of God and Texas!"

That's a passel of killing, Davy Crockett thought. Soberfaced as a hungry hound dog, he listened, and it appeared that he was hanging on each word. His course through politics was littered with the forms of spellbinders like Travis, who had tried to smother old Davy with words; but he had no doubt of the man's sincerity and his will to fight.

"We stand before the bar of hard decision," Travis said.

That was backed by the almost simultaneous roar of a half dozen cannon.

"I will not try to mislead you with any further hope that we will be reinforced. I ask you now to look into your own hearts and make the final choice."

With a dramatic gesture Travis drew his sword. He walked down the ramp and his men parted to make him a path. He waved them toward the front of the church and they fell back. And then he dragged the point of his sword along the hard-packed dirt and there it was—a line, a choice.

"Let no man feel that censure will fall upon him if he chooses to leave this fort. Those who find reason to do so can go with my good wishes and the blessings of their comrades."

Travis paused.

"All those who choose to stay, to give, if necessary, their lives to the cause of freedom on the sacred soil of Texas, come forward across this line!"

For a long moment no one moved.

Tapley Holland, age twenty-four, was the first to cross the

line and stand by Travis. They came then by groups, volunteers and regulars mingling in the companionship of war.

From his cot Jim Bowie said, "Boys, I can't make it myself, so I'd appreciate it if some of you gave me a hand."

Crockett grinned and grabbed one corner of the cot. A dozen men leaped to help carry Bowie across the line. And then but for one man they were all with Travis.

Louis Rose, who had chewed the bitter meat of defeat on Napoleon's retreat from Moscow, and at Waterloo, sank down on his heels and held his face in his hands. Someone began to urge him to rise and join the rest. Crockett said, "Be still! Moses there may be the only smart coon in the whole damned place!"

Rose stood up. He wavered for a moment longer—and then he walked out of the church.

It was growing dusk as they went back to their posts.

"You know everything, Hawkins," Billy Wells said. "What's 'by esplanade'?"

"When the buggers climb up the walls on ladders."

"They ain't none on the outside."

"They'll bring their own," McGregor said.

At the angling barricade out from the church, Dr. Thompson chuckled as he stood beside Crockett. "All the time in there I kept thinking of something you did once when you were running for Congress.

"You were stumping and there was a real orating fellow running against you. He spoke first, a mighty fine speech about solving all kinds of problems. Then you got up, looking awkward and silly, with a coonskin in your hand. You shuffled forward a little, grinned, and then you stroked the pelt and said, 'Now ain't that a mighty fine piece of fur?'"

"I remember," Crockett said, chuckling. "That was all I said and I won that district easy."

"For God and Crockett and Tennessee," Thompson said, and they both laughed heartily.

That night John Smith went out with official messages and personal letters. So tight was the investment by the enemy that Travis doubted that Smith would make it. An hour later he sent two more men, Byrd Lockhart and Andy Sowell.

Two hours later he sent the last courier to leave the Alamo, little Jim Allen.

After midnight, some of the Gonzales, led by Lieutenant Kimbell, went over the north wall and made a sally to knock out the advanced battery.

They got in close and killed some of the enemy, but the emplacement was swarming with Mexican soldiers, and the two flanking cannons opened up. The raiders came back without losing a man, but they had been unable to still the dangerous battery.

Louis Rose was gone then. He dropped over the wall with a bundle of his possessions and went in a direction which he reasoned the Mexicans would least expect a man from the Alamo to take. He went west, toward Bexar.

Sent by old Veedor Bustamente to warn the North Americans that an attack was due at dawn, Bernal got only a hundred yards from the river before a Mexican sentry caught him. "Aha! And where does this one go?"

Bernal hung his head. "I have great hunger."

"So! And now you come to steal from soldiers whose pay is twelve and a half cents a day, when they are paid at all."

"But I am hungry, my lieutenant."

"I am a sergeant, as anyone can see—if it were daylight." Having been very alert in catching this young thief, the sergeant now lectured him. "And from this pay soldiers must buy their own food. Did you know that?"

"No, my sergeant."

"Well, it is so, and you would steal from them. Who sent you, little thief?"

"No one sent me, my sergeant. There was no food in the house, and I had great hunger."

"Everyone has great hunger, but that is no reason to steal, do you understand?"

"Yes, my sergeant."

"Hunger is a terrible thing. I have been hungry most of my life." The sergeant took from his shirt two tortillas which he had accepted as a bribe from a *zapadore* who had begged to carry water to the cannons, instead of being sent forward to dig in a place where the bullets of the North Americans had killed many men.

"Here, little thief. Now go before I take them back and devour them at one gulp!" The sergeant cursed the poor ones of Mexico, since he was of them himself.

Bernal went home. He was afraid to waken Veedor and tell him of the failure, so he ate the tortillas and went to bed with

130

his six brothers, In the morning, when there was no dawn attack, Bernal was able to say that he indeed had gone to the Alamo and warned them.

"You are brave," said Veedor. "You are the only one of all my worthless descendants who is like me."

And a terrible liar on top of that, Bernal thought.

CHAPTER 18

BEFORE THE NORTH wall collapsed, Dick Starr took his trophy of war, his lance, and drove it into the top of the breastworks back from the wall. Let 'em, by God, come and get it!

For almost a fourth of its length, beginning at the northeast corner, the wall was down, a pile of tumbled masonry that had been gathered rock by rock long ago by Coahuiltecan slave laborers under the watchful eyes of Franciscans.

And then all cannonading by the Mexicans ceased. The sudden stillness was a thing to wonder at. It hurt the ears.

"They're going to make their rush now," Bourne told Starr. "That's what they're going to do."

Everyone thought so. But there was no rush. Couriers came and went, to and from, the headquarters of Santa Anna, no more, it seemed, than before. The Texans realized, too, that even the musket fire had ceased.

Splashes of earth on the tops of trenches and embankments showed that the *zapadores* were still digging, extending their works toward the fort, but nowhere could the defenders see any evidence that battalions of infantry were forming for an assault.

The silence began to hit them hard. They drooped at their posts, dozing, rousing suddenly with the sensation of hearing shouts and cannonading, but there was only quiet; and then they dozed again, closer than ever to the deep, dark sleep of exhaustion.

Even at the breached wall there was no musket fire. Major Jameson ordered riflemen to the cannon ramps inside to pick off any eager musket men who tried to break the sudden peace, and then he directed a party of defenders trying to repair the wall.

All they could do was raise it a few inches along its length,

131

and they knew that the advanced cannon could knock down their work in no time, but they had to try.

Carlos Espalier, seventeen, of Bexar, was in the work party. He was horrified when they found the bodies of two *zapadores* who had been killed when they crept up the night before to spy out the breastworks beyond the wall.

"Let's put them right in with the rocks," said one of the New Orleans volunteers.

And that was done.

Young Carlos kept looking at the bare feet of the dead men, tough callused feet that had followed ploughs in some poor field behind a burro, and now they were being covered by hard rocks. Carlos had seen feet like those all his life. Suddenly he felt terrible anger against all the bad things that happened forever in Mexico, but, not understanding them, his rage narrowed like a dagger to one man, Santa Anna.

He dreamed of killing him, but he knew that El Presidente would not come through that breach while fighting was going on; so Carlos transferred his hate to those whom Santa Anna would send, even though they would be poor men with feet like those among the rocks.

They carried Jim Bowie to a little room at the front of the church, leaving him with Ham, whose eyes rolled with fear because he knew what the moving meant. On a stool beside the bed Crockett laid Bowie's pistols, charged and primed.

"If the time comes, Ham, put them in his hands."

Ham nodded soundlessly.

Gunner Hutchinson leaned against the eighteen-pounder and found himself dozing. Goddamn the quietness! He shook his head and stared blearily toward Bexar and the *jacals* that lay between.

What a time he'd had over there! A week before this scrape started, he'd been discharged, but he'd stayed on because he had no place to go. And now he was in the Alamo.

"You did put grape in Old Twister, didn't you?" he asked the loader. Because of one weak wheel, the piece always recoiled to the side, and that was why they had given it the name.

"Huh?" the loader asked, yawning.

"Yeah, he did," said the spongeman, Linn. "Damn it, stop gaping your mouth! You're making me do it too."

132

The gunners at the pieces behind the lunette outside the fort debated about taking two rows of earth-filled bags off the barricade in the porte-cochere. It was a hard scramble to get over the top of that barrier in a hurry.

While they were still discussing the subject, Lieutenant Evans came out and said, "Put another row on top, boys."

"Jesus, we can hardly squeeze through there now!"

"If you have to, you'll dive through a knothole like weasels. Don't forget, I want the guns spiked first."

"I wisht they come now, by Glory. I cain't stay awake much longer."

On the west wall, the little group that centered around the likeable Mark Hawkins and his long bombs were talking to keep awake.

"How long since we had coffee?" Wilson asked.

"I ain't had none since we come in here," Wells said. "I don't drink it. Now about these here ladders——"

"There's a lad I'd like to take back to Ireland with me—if I ever go," said Hawkins. "He'd confuse the best wits in Dublin."

"Some of the officers still got coffee," Wilson said. "I seen Captain——"

"Give me no tales about the officers," McGregor said. "If they've got champagne, I'm for them. When it comes to sleeping, they've had less than any of us."

"Champagne?" Wells frowned. "Does it taste like rum?"

"In a way," Hawkins answered. "It happens that I have a few bottles of it left in my pack in the barracks. Shall we go sample it?"

"No fooling!" Wells cried.

McGregor clucked his tongue. "Lad, lad! After all the blather this bog-trotter has given you . . ."

"How do I know?" Wells protested. "Mark is always up to something. He had a whole sackful of rum buried by an outhouse over in Bexar, so I thought maybe——"

"It's still there." Hawkins sighed. "When this little Donnybrook is over, we'll bite the ends from the bottles and guzzle it to the last drop."

"About these here ladders they're going to bring," Wells said, "how's the best way to spill 'em?"

"If they stick above the wall——" McGregor pointed to some
133

planks he had carried up that morning. He made a shoving motion.

Hawkins said, "And if they don't stick up that far, Billy me bye, you must wait till they're fully loaded with climbing buggers and then you must leap down gracefully and pull the bottom away with a monstrous jerk."

Their tiredness made it extra funny. Wilson lay on his side and laughed until tears came.

The first cannon shot that broke the stillness came from the north battery. Men who had relaxed were suddenly jerked back to reality with the shock of the gun.

It might be the prelude to heavy artillery fire that would end just before an infantry rush.

Travis thought so himself. He rushed from headquarters buttoning his coat.

Peace was gone. Tired, jerking nerves once more had to go to work, filtering impressions, steeling men for the supreme effort Travis had talked about.

More cannons fired, but after a time it was apparent that nothing much was happening. Then the artillery slackened off. It grew desultory. Santa Anna played his war of nerves with fiendish skill. All day long the Mexican guns fired just enough to keep the men of the Alamo from getting any extended period of rest.

In quick surges the gunners hit their sodden nerves, drove them awake, then let them sag back, then roused them with another quick-timed burst of fire.

What repair work had been done on the north wall was ruined. Major Jameson didn't bother to try again.

By early afternoon, General Santa Anna had issued secret orders to all his top commanders. In conference preceding that, Generals Cos and Duque and Castrillon had most politely, but firmly, protested their leader's intentions to storm the Alamo at this time.

One wall had been breached, but that was no great victory. Deadly riflemen and belching cannon would cover that breach. Was it not better to wait, Castrillon said, until the twelve-pound guns now on the way arrived? Then all the walls could be systematically destroyed without great loss of life.

No, it was not better to wait! said El Presidente, his pale, handsome face flushed with irritation.

134

General Cos, brother-in-law of the great one, made no more objections. He shrugged within himself. They were all like that, these dictators. In haste they must act, even though it was wrong and many lives needlessly sacrificed.

But still they must act, always they must do something hard and dramatic, or their power soon waned.

"This miserable mission fort, built only to withstand Indians, has resisted a great army for twelve days," Santa Anna said bitterly. "But for it and the rebellious dogs who hold it, foreigners and vile adventurers all, I would now be north of the Sabine and this rebellion would be settled in the blood of those who have defied the Supreme Government."

And that is you, thought Cos, looking straight ahead.

Santa Anna dismissed them by rising.

His clerks wrote the order:

For the private information of Generals of Division and Corps Commanders:

. . . His Excellency, the Chief in General, directs that by four o'clock tomorrow morning the attacking columns shall be stationed within gunshot of the first line of entrenchments for the purpose of making the assault, upon the signal given by His Excellency, which will be the sounding of a bugle from the north battery . . .

. . . The General in Chief will, at the proper time, designate the points against which the attacking columns will perform . . .

. . . The first column will be provided with ten scaling ladders, two crow bars and two axes. The second . . . with the same quantity; the third with six; the fourth with two. Men carrying ladders will sling their muskets over their shoulders . . . All caps will be provided with chin straps . . .

. . . The men composing the attacking column will retire to rest at sundown, preparatory to moving at midnight . . .

. . . Arms, particularly bayonets, will be put in the best condition . . . When the moon rises the musketeers of the San Luis battalion . . . will retire to their quarters . . . Other units will retire at sundown . . .

. . . The cavalry will saddle . . . at three o'clock in the morning. It will be their duty to watch camp and to prevent the escape of anyone . . .

The eyes of General Don Francisco Duque blazed when he

135

read about the duty of the cavalry. *To prevent the escape of anyone.* Indeed! To cut down the infantry that turned back from the murderous fire they would have to face. It was an insult to declare before the fact that brave men must be crowded by the cavalry.

The devil strike those Cossacks of General Sesma's, who did nothing but ride about the country like lords, and who could not even prevent the going and coming of couriers at the Alamo. Let hell receive them without Grace.

General Duque's second column, including three companies of the San Luis battalion of volunteers, would go forward well, he vowed, and he would lead them. And if some of them turned and ran, it would not be because they were cowards that needed watching by the cursed cavalry, but because all men are heroes and cowards in one.

10:00 P.M. The cannons ceased firing. It was no momentary pause this time. An hour passed. The quiet was unbroken. Another hour. The men of the Alamo felt themselves sagging from the reaction of stillness. Midnight. The encircling army was deathly quiet.

Outposts south and west of the Alamo, three men who had been sent to their quarters in the afternoon to get rest to hold them through their lonely vigil, which was to end at 2:00 when others came out to relieve them, fought hard to stay alert. It was agony to do so when all was strangely hushed.

At the corner of a rock *jacal* south of the fort, Nemesio de Oca lay on his belly and waited. He was a Lipan scout who for three days had lived by himself on the San Antonio, well removed from the army.

Now his nose was cleared of the odors of men that would have clogged it if he had stayed with the other scouts and soldiers. He could smell keenly everything at came on the still night air. By this and other senses attuned to the dark, he had determined where two of the outposts lay. The third one he would find when the time came.

By the promise of El Presidente himself, Nemesio would be released from the army to go back to his people if he did well what he was supposed to do.

He had no hate for North Americans. He scarcely knew them. They were all going to die anyway, those three outside the fort and all the rest inside.

It would be a favor, then, to the first three if they died soundlessly, suffering but an instant. And it would free Nemesio from the army.

He sniffed the odor of the fort. It was of oldness, and of dust, and of freshly turned damp earth, and of the stink of men, and of buckets of cannon water rank with the deadness of burned powder, and of cows that had been killed by the night fire of scouts. It all mingled strangely in Nemesio's nostrils.

It was of death.

CHAPTER 19

COLONEL WILLIAM BARRETT TRAVIS stood alone on a gun platform at the north wall, staring desperately into the night. The quietness was a blessing and a terrible threat. They would come by that breach where the bodies of two men were already stinking horribly.

They would come from all directions, he thought dully. The depression of stillness crushed against him hard. He could no longer argue with himself. The Alamo was lost. And the high, unlimited future that he had planned for himself in Texas was lost too.

He went slowly back to his quarters. It was a pity before God that so few men in the fort understood the things that they were dying for. He had tried to tell them but he knew that few had grasped his principles.

They were here, and they had stayed here, from pride of race, from a heritage of being free, wild and without discipline, because of friendship with each other, and because they knew they couldn't live before other men if they quit a fight.

At the doorway of his quarters, Travis stopped and looked at the quiet, sleeping fort. His sodden spirit flared.

They could win even yet! From what he had learned of the men of the Alamo, a miracle was not impossible.

McGregor gnawed a piece of hard cornbread. His jaws moved slower and slower and then there was a swallow that he held in his mouth as his head fell forward. He woke only because of the pain in his neck, sometime later.

137

The rest of them were all sound asleep.

Angrily, McGregor crumbled some of the cornbread in his hands and rubbed it into his eyes. The gritty meal burned like the fires of hell. He took a deep breath, blinking as his eyes began to stream water, fighting to keep from rubbing them.

He kept awake.

Once he thought he heard a soft noise somewhere between the west wall and the first entrenchments. He strained to see until misty shapes and shadowy forms that he knew were not real moved before his aching eyes.

It was deathly quiet again.

McGregor would never know that he actually had heard a soft noise as he thought. It was the death kick of Asa Walker, twenty-three, who never even woke when Nemesio de Oca completed the task that would release him from the army.

When they actually came into the perimeter of McGregor's vision, barely seen by the light of a pale, dying moon, he could not believe his eyes at first. He waited one moment longer.

There they were! A long row of pale pantaloons that seemed to be floating along the ground.

"Mexicans! Attack! Attack!"

Wilson, Hawkins, Wells and all the other defenders of the west wall roused, their sleep-drugged minds reacting to the threat and putting weapons in their hands before they were fully awake.

Then from the north came a burst of cheering as one of the Mexican columns released the tension of a long wait lying on the ground.

A bugle screamed one high clear note.

"Hold your fire, byes," Hawkins said calmly. "And for Christ's sake, get down!"

In the stunned moments of first awakening, many of them had leaped up. All along the barracks roof cool heads like Hawkins brought them back to their senses. They dropped again behind the bags of earth and waited.

Only two or three fired before they had sure marks.

The cannons of the Alamo began to boom on all sides. Billy Wells heard the loud roar of the eighteen-pounder as it hurled grape at the oncoming line, and then there was a gap where men had been cut to pieces. Again the big gun and the twelve-pounder near the center of the wall whipped grape into the Mexicans. They kept coming.

138

"Give it to them, I think," Sergeant Hersee said coolly.

Wells already had a form in his sights. He fired. The man went down. A line of musket fire winked all at once. Wells didn't hear a ball strike, although one had thudded into the bag, close to his head.

Wells rolled on his back and reloaded. He fired and saw a soldier stumble to his knees; and then he saw the ladders Hawkins had talked about, borne by four men trotting in advance of the infantry.

He was reloading the third time when he realized that everyone near him was doing the same as he, firing, recharging, firing again. Till then the fight had been a personal affair between him and each target. He rolled over and fired at one of the ladder men, who dropped. The musket on his shoulder flew free and stood upright as the long bayonet stuck in the ground.

When Wells was ready to fire again, all the ladder men were down. He picked an officer, a tall man who was half turned, waving his command on.

They were so close now that Wells grabbed his pistols and fired into the general mass. They were wavering. By Jeems they were! Tall cockades on the ground. Blue-coated forms outstretched. A man was crawling, clutching ahead with one hand, his face looking back toward the wall.

Two men were carrying a ladder away. They both went down, and two more grabbed it.

Sullenly, defiantly, the Mexicans faded back into the dawn, no longer a line but a disordered mass. The west wall cannons chased them into their entrenchments.

Hawkins said, "Sure now, we did ourselves proud, we did."

All three of Wells' weapons were empty. He was reloading them as fast as he could when he realized that there was fighting at other places around the Alamo.

And he heard for the first time the playing of the massed bands still urging the Mexicans on.

Asleep at the eight-pounders near the breached north wall, Dan Bourne and Dick Starr staggered to their feet when they heard the shouting on the west wall. They ran to their firing ramps when they heard the cheering of the Mexicans.

Travis reached the north batteries soon afterward, yelling, "Give them hell, men!" He ran to the battery that had been swung to rake the breach.

Just before the cannons fired their first charge, Bourne

139

licked his lips and said, "They look like ghosts out there."

And then they were close, their cotton pants flapping, and pale light on their bayonets, and men in front with ladders. Bourne killed a ladder-bearer. The rush behind rolled over the man. He saw an officer holding his sword above his head, and marked him for his second shot.

But Starr felled the man while Bourne was recharging.

A shower of grape went whistling through the breach. Bourne heard the screaming of soldiers on the ground, mixing with the wailing of the bands and the crackle of rifle fire beside him.

One-Eye Guerrero knew that music. The *deguello,* the fire and death call, the cry of beheading. Blood and killing. The Spanish had played it against the Moors in ancient times. It cried out murder.

It ran wildly through his blood, but it didn't affect his hands nor his one good eye. He shot an officer, picking him with cool deliberation among the mass of targets.

Almost together the eight-pounders rocked again and jagged death struck the soldiers. Guerrero killed with his next shot a man who had already turned to run. He cursed himself for doing so.

Out there the high hats swirled and bobbed. The soldiers fired a ragged volley as they ran. To reload they must stop, Guerrero thought wickedly. But they were shouted on by officers, including one who raised himself from the ground to wave his sword.

Cannon fire broke them. Rifles shot them dead. They slowed, their bayonets worthless. Another volley from the guns tore them cruelly.

Back, back . . . they turned once more to men, from heroes. They ran from the merciless rain of death, and, in their going, their hard bare feet and their *guaraches* trampled the life from the wounded General Duque who had led them even as he had vowed he would lead them.

"We licked them!" Bourne cried, knowing only what every man in battle knows: that small part directly before him.

He swung toward Starr. Starr was slumped against the wall with blood on his face and across his feet lay Spain Summerlin, nineteen, who never again would brag of Tennessee.

"Why—why, they didn't even shoot at us!" Bourne cried.

"They shoot plenty much," Guerrero said. "You damn' right they shoot."

At the south wall there was still fighting, but Bourne scarcely paid any attention as he kept staring at Starr and Summerlin.

The gunners behind their lunette at the south wall were ready to turn and dive over the barricade behind them. They had ripped five rounds into the ranks coming at them from the dark, and now there wasn't time to reload.

And then it happened there too. Riflemen on the low building and Crockett's men, firing obliquely from their barricade, broke the charge and the Mexicans streamed back to their defenses.

The *deguello* ceased. The men of the Alamo cheered, yelling for themselves and for each other. On west and east and north and south they had repulsed the enemy.

Walking back after all their men had fled, Lieutenant Alonzo Hernandez and Sergeant Archuleta of the Matamoros Battalion stepped around the figures writhing and moaning on the ground.

"Again?" the sergeant asked.

"Yes! When we are reformed, of course again, you idiot."

CHAPTER 20

"GOD HELP US, we're out of powder!" Micajah Autry cried. He ran to the lunette and grabbed his rifle.

In the flat light of early daybreak the second attack was coming at them, so close now that there would not have been time to reload the piece anyway.

With his back to the enemy, a ball of grape poised to ram into the muzzle, Pete Bailey looked over his shoulder. He could see faces behind the bayonets. He dropped the ball and leaped to get his rifle.

The other four-pounder fired a raking blast belly-high into the soldiers, and then the gunners snatched up small arms. The charge veered away, to the sides of the lunette.

When their rifles and pistols were empty, the gunners retreated into the porte-cochere, scrambling over the bags of dirt that almost blocked the entrance.

Autry thought he was the last one but when he pivoted on his belly atop the barricade he saw that Bailey had stayed behind to drive a soft iron wedge into the touch-hole of the battery.

"Let it go, Pete!" Autry yelled.

Bailey drove the spike. He grabbed his rifle. As he turned to run two soldiers charged around the end of the lunette. Bailey swung to face them, lifting his rifle as a club. Their bayonets drove into him.

"Get out of the way!" someone snarled at Autry, and fired a rifle above his legs.

One soldier dropped before his bayonet was withdrawn. The other was killed by two men who fired at the same time.

Hell was roaring on top of the low building above Autrey's head. Two scaling ladders had been placed against the wall, but no one reached the top of the ladders. Men leaned out and fired point blank into the faces of those trying to climb, and others on the wall broke the ranks of the soldiers coming up to support their hapless comrades.

Once more the attack reeled back from the south buildings.

At the angling barricade, held to be the most vulnerable point in all the defenses, the Tennesseans had littered the ground with soldiers, and the four cannons there had torn the heart out of the charge directed at that point.

Crockett looked over the barricade as the assault broke and fell away. "I guess we fed 'em snakes, boys!"

Once more the men of the Alamo had reason to cheer, but they were too weary to do it.

The attack at the north had been hurled back. On east and west the assaults had failed a second time. In leaving the field the troops on both the long sides of the Alamo had hugged the walls as far as they could before they had to break into the open, and both forces had veered northward when they retired.

That was something that did not go unnoticed at Santa Anna's headquarters, now only a little more than a quarter of a mile northwest of the fort.

"Seven dead and six wounded," Espallier reported to Travis at the batteries near the north wall. "Can we hold them a third time, Colonel?"

"We can! We must!"

Lieutenant Evans came up, his eyes red-rimmed, his mouth hanging from near exhaustion. "Our powder supply is almost gone, Colonel Travis."

For the last time Travis looked east, thinking bitterly of all the appeals he had made for men, powder and provisions. "Do the best you can, Lieutenant."

Dickerson came down from the platform on the chapel, where he had been watching activity to the south, and all the while hoping against hope that they wouldn't come again.

But he had seen them regrouping their shattered forces, bringing up reserves. Reserves! Where were the Texas reserves they had begged and prayed for?

He too had looked east from the chapel.

With Angelina in her arms, his wife came from the room where the women had taken safety during the assaults. She asked a question without speaking.

He tried to smile. "We've beat them off twice. They'll think a long time before they come again." And then he bent to kiss his child, and walked away quickly.

Wilson rested his head on his arms. "Christ, I'm tired. When this is over, I'm going to sleep for a week."

"What kind of sleep?" someone asked dully.

"You think they're going to come again?" Billy Wells asked Hawkins.

For once there was no humor in Hawkins. "Yes," he said. He rose and put his three musket-bombs in a row, arranging them so that they all lay evenly aligned. He pressed the fuses that ran from the primed pans against the roof and carefully poured powder around the ends of each fuse.

They watched him curiously, half angered by his slow deliberateness.

"You wasted a lot of time on those goddamn things!" Wilson said.

"Maybe." Hawkins lay down and closed his eyes.

McGregor had developed a twitch on the right side of his face. He kept rubbing it as he looked with one eye at the mustering of forces for a new attack, and then the whole scene dissolved and he saw with breath-taking clearness mists rising from the lakes of his childhood, and the heather running down from rocky heights.

"There's no green here like there is in Scotland," he said, not realizing that he was going to speak aloud.

"Aye," Wilson said softly, knowing exactly what McGregor meant.

Some of them fell asleep while waiting for the next assault.

143

It came· as it had before, from all directions, and once more the men of the Alamo dragged from their tortured bodies the energy to meet it.

A second cannon had been brought down to cover the breach in the north wall, ranged beside the first one, behind the breastworks in the plaza, and there also was most of the gallant band of men from Gonzales. Johnny Kellogg, Isaac Millsaps, John Cane, Galba Fuqua, age sixteen, and all the rest, with Lieutenant Kimbell lying beside them.

A third time the *deguello* cried for blood.

They came on without yelling this time, grim and driven men who knew that the foremost of them would die. Behind them, like grinning jackals, the cavalry waited for those who would try to leave the blood-soaked field.

Travis was at the lone eight-pounder on the platform. It threw death three times into the Mexican ranks before the rush of men was in so close that the piece could not be depressed to hit them.

The men of Gonzales, and men on the firing ramps along the walls, shot blue-coated soldiers by squads as soon as they came in range, and the two guns at the breastworks hurled iron through the breach with screaming fury.

The north end held. Those who tried to cross the rubble of the barricade fell among the rocks.

For the third time the charge wavered.

It was then that those who had attacked from the east and west sides followed their orders and their officers and swung around the north end of the Alamo to add two more columns to the crushing weight of the Toluca Battalion, which was bearing the frightful brunt of the attack.

Some of the reserves came in.

Sergeant Panfilio Olid, waiting with his cavalry troop, saw clearly what happened then.

By weight of mass the charge was carried forward, but Merciful Christ! They were killing each other, that infantry. They fired as they ran, from excitement and fear, with the blood cry of the *deguello* hammering in their brains.

They were men not long used to muskets. The rear ranks fired too low, into the backs of their comrades, and some of those in the crush ahead also fired wildly, shooting the men of the Toluca Battalion.

144

It was not enough that the North Americans were slaughtering them, Panfilio thought, they had to murder each other. That was the infantry for you.

Ladders went against the wall west of the breach, at least fifteen of them, and men were literally pushed against them to start climbing. When their heads rose above the wall, the climbers, helpless in the last moment of scrambling to get atop the wall, were killed instantly. They fell back and crashed on those starting to climb.

But there were many of them and they were brave men. They kept trying. Bourne and others along firing platforms killed them with rifle shots, with pistol shots, with clubbed rifles, and then with rocks when the rifles broke.

Men in buckskin tomahawked them or ripped them with big knives. A few soldiers reached the top of the wall, but they did not live.

To lean out in order to fire down into the mass of men against the wall was death to any defender who tried it, because hundreds of musket balls came sweeping like hail when any Texan showed his head. Pat Herndon, Domingo Losoyo and Andres Nava died that way, too anxious in their lust for blood.

Bourne lived because he knew where one of the ladders was. He concentrated on that one place, killing anyone who put his head above the wall.

Travis left the cannon on the platform. It was out of powder and it could not have been serviced anyway because of the musket fire concentrated on it. He went to one of the pieces at the breastworks.

Quickly, he sized up the situation. They were holding at the north. For God and Texas they were holding! He saw a bitter fight in progress on the roof of the south building; even as he looked, the defenders cleared the rooftop of soldiers.

There was no break-through at the barricade. He could hear the four-pounders there still churning hate and destruction.

The west wall still held, although the defenders had thinned along it, running northward on the building to help repel the attack at the breach.

From the courtyard of the church, the east wall was the strongest part of the Alamo, with its long two-story barracks, the convent yard behind, and its solid line of firing platform north from the barracks to the breach.

145

After one glance Travis wasted no more time on the east defenses. He fired his rifle into the rush against the breach, and shouted, "Give them hell, boys!"

The boys were doing that, the gunners at their pieces, the deadly fighters of Gonzales, and the riflemen who had come down from the east wall to reinforce those at the breastworks—and who, unknowingly, had left a fatal soft spot by doing so.

Mark Hawkins and Sergeant Hersee had tried to stem the drift of defenders northward on the west wall buildings.

"Hold your places here!" they cried, but the heavy action was north, while the rush against the west wall had dwindled off with unexpected weakness, and so too many of the riflemen went north, and there were too few of them in the first place.

When the first cockades rose above the west wall, Hawkins and the few who had remained blew the wearers back upon the soldiers below. And then more and more cockades rose up.

Billy Wells and Wilson and a few more saw the trouble and came running back from the north. With weapons, planks, knives and stones, they beat the climbers back.

They held that wall by spotting the points where the ladders were and by savagely destroying every man who tried to come over and walk upon their roof.

Hawkins then found time to strike fire to his first long bomb. He pitched it over where he knew a ladder leaned against the wall. It did not explode.

The next two did, and though the powder was weak and dirty, the screams and moans that followed the explosions told him that he had not wasted his time.

McGregor blew apart the pale, determined face of a captain as he rose above the wall, clutching with one hand and raising a pistol with the other. "Get the next one, Hawkins!" he cried, and began to recharge his pistols.

We've held them for the third time! Travis told himself. They were wavering at the breach. If they fell back this time, he doubted that their officers could rally them again.

And then he saw the fatal cracking on the east wall, north from the corner of the long barracks. Too many men had left there. Too many ladders had been thrown up. The Mexicans

146

were on the wall, coming over, driving back or bayoneting the few defenders.

Travis struck Lieutenant Kimbell on the shoulder and pointed, and Kimbell scrambled along the breastworks, shaking men from their concentration on the breach and directing them to fire against the new threat.

For perhaps one minute the fate of the Alamo was suspended by events on that section of the east wall running north from the barracks. Kimbell fell with a musket ball in his heart. Isaac Millsaps went down trying to relay the lieutenant's orders. But for that, the north end might have held a little longer.

But the defenders were too few. Mexican soldiers came over the wall. Each ladder spouted men. They were inside the fort at last. They had the men at the breastworks under fire from the side and from the rear. The cannoneers began to fall.

Fire covering the breach slackened. Bayonets flashed as blue-coated soldiers came stumbling through over the bodies of their own dead. Some of those first men died, but the pressure behind sent more and more.

Like sheep pouring over a low fence the Mexican column came over the broken north wall, and then they had the men on the roof of the west building at their mercy.

Screaming faces. White cross belts. The Sabbath sun on flashing bayonets. Muskets pounding fire. All the hatred backed up by long days of futile trying. Irresistible numbers.

And the *deguello* calling fire and death.

Colonel Travis saw the end. He drew his good bright sword. He raised it in both hands and broke it over the hot cannon barrel. He flung the haft at the surging mass. He drew his pistol.

He never lived to see the most savage part of all the fighting.

CHAPTER 21

THE WEST DEFENSES gave way next. Ed Nelson and Charlie Haskell fell as they were reloading their pistols. McGregor saw blood on their backs. He threw a startled look behind him. He saw where the musket balls had come from.

147

The whole north end of the plaza was lost.

So savagely dedicated to killing climbers were some of the west wall defenders that they had to be struck hard on the shoulders and turned before they grasped what was happening behind them. They began to jump to the plaza.

When McGregor struck the ground, his foot turned on a rock. His right leg went under him and his weight came down on it. He heard the bone break and when he looked, it was sticking out through his thigh. One pistol was still in his hand. He rolled on his side and crawled to retrieve the other one, which had been jarred from his grip by the fall.

He saw the rush of white and blue going down the plaza. The men who had come off the roof with him were running into the buildings at his back.

He had jumped between two doors. Either one was too far to drag himself. The doorways closed even as he thought of trying. He looked at his pistols. They were both charged.

Then Hawkins came from somewhere and grabbed him under the arm and started to lift him. "Noo, noo!" McGregor cried.

Three screaming soldiers veered from the rush and came at them. McGregor shot one of them in the stomach. Hawkins parried a bayonet thrust with his rifle, then drove the butt of it with crushing force into the throat of the second man.

Astride McGregor's legs, Hawkins grunted as he swung the rifle against the head of the third man. "We'll give them a bit of Irish hell," he said, as if he were sitting on the roof tinkering with his long bombs. He dragged McGregor against the wall.

The rush of bayonets came at them. Mark Hawkins swung his rifle, beating and clubbing. It was knocked from his hands. He ripped a man with his knife and held to him while he reached and slashed another one in the throat. He was still swinging the knife when the bayonets pinned him from three sides.

McGregor saw the sharp points dip toward him. He threw his empty pistol. With the thatches of his ruddy brows drawn down and a snarl on his lips, he shot a soldier who had lost his tall hat in the rush.

The bayonets were streaks of hotness, not hurting greatly. McGregor hammered in the head of a youthful soldier who had been knocked to his knees beside the sitting Scot. He tried to raise the pistol again, but it fell from his grip.

He heard the sound of bagpipes as his head fell forward; and the maddened soldiers continued to stab him.

148

The south end gave way last. It had to go when its defenders saw the hordes of Mexican soldiers filling the whole north end of the plaza, with hundreds more streaming over the undefended walls and through the breach.

Crockett swung half of his men from the barricade to try to stem the southern rush at the low courtyard wall. Too few of them to start. The division weakened the defense at the barricade. Survivors of the Mexican column that had strewn the ground with their dead before the barricade, and then had fallen back to the shelter of stone *jacals* south of the Alamo now rushed the barricade.

Two of the four-pound batteries fired one last round. The surviving gunners ran for the chapel. The doors were closed in the faces of the last few men falling back from the breastworks.

The Crockett men at the south end of the low wall retired into the granary, and Crockett with them. From the doorway they cut down Mexicans with every shot. The courtyard before the chapel was a milling mass of soldiery.

On the roof of the chapel, Colonel Bonham had worked the gun crews like fiends in the lapses between the three assaults. He had mounted one of the twelve-pounders at the southwest corner of the chapel where there was yet cemented timbers covering the small rooms below.

Point blank into the yelling Mexicans the gunners hurled a charge of scrap that raked the courtyard with horrible results. Before they could fire a second blast, the eighteen-pounder cut in from the southwest angle of the plaza. Hutchinson and the gunners there had turned the piece with the desperate energy of men who would not quit.

They tore soldiers swarming in the plaza to shreds.

Then Bonham hit them again.

From the doorway of the granary, Crockett saw the four-pounder being trained to blast the building. With him were Micajah Autry, Dr. Thompson, Purdy Reynolds and a few others.

"We've got to get that gun, boys," Crockett said.

The battery on the church and the second, and final, blast from the eighteen-pounder gave them their chance. They rushed out and killed the Mexican gunners, catching them cold by the sudden sortie.

But when they tried to fight their way back to the granary, they were trapped by twenty or thirty soldiers who had torn the bags away in the porte-cochere and rushed into the plaza.

Crockett's little band fought like catamounts, ripping and yelling; like bears, clubbing and growling; like fiends from hell, roaring their defiance—like Tennesseans.

One by one they went down, with a ring of dead around them. Crockett was alone. In awe some of the soldiers fell back from him, this terrible man whose cap of fur swung its tail as he swung his weapons, a rifle in his right hand, a great knife in his left. Red-eyed and roaring, he didn't wait for them to come to him; he went after them.

But not too many watched in awe. There were others who hated this fearsome man above all others in the fort. He had stood on the walls, insulting them, killing them with fiendish accuracy, laughing at their musket shots.

Vizente Zambrano broke his right arm with a musket shot. Simon Escamilla bayoneted him in the left shoulder, and had his guts ripped upward even as he made the lunge.

Blood-greasy, the left arm still wielded the knife. It took the lives of Jose Gotari and Ignacio Albrego. Someone shot the monster in the chest, and still he would not die. He spun around and a soldier lunging at him with a bayonet drove it into the throat of a comrade.

Crockett lost the knife when it was wrenched away by a soldier who fell sidewise with the steel in his rib cage. As the bayonets drove into him from all sides, Davy Crockett seized a man by the throat and killed him with one hand.

When he went down at last, those who had stood back in awe now came forward with mad shouts to help mutilate his body.

The fight was far from being finished.

Dead lay Gunner Hutchinson and all but one of his crew at the silent eighteen-pounder. Dead was the gallant Bonham across the gun he had fired twice from the chapel roof, with the gunners dead around the piece, or else driven back along the platforms inside the chapel, from where they were still picking off soldiers in the convent yard and south and east of the church.

Across the trail of the overrun battery at the north lay Colonel Travis, a pistol ball in his head.

Face down in the plaza lay Evans, who had been running desperately to fire the Mexican powder in the sacristy of the church when he was struck.

150

A few lay dead upon the roofs, and along the fronts of the buildings lay men like McGregor, who had not been able to get inside, and Hawkins, who had chosen to go down while standing over a comrade.

No North American was alive in the plaza.

But every building held them, trapped and cornered—and still defiant. They knew their fate. They were going to make the Mexican army pay another river of blood to get them from those buildings.

From the chapel they continued to kill; from the roof of the long barracks they still sent death, and out of the windows and loopholes, disdaining even yet to wound, shooting only for the head.

From a window in the upper story of the long barracks, Guerrero and Juan Abamillo fired carefully and steadily. They called the soldiers lovers of dogs and other animals, seducers of their mothers, betrayers of their sisters, murderers of their infants conceived by sodomy—and many other names more vile.

Less eloquent, the Texans called the soldiers sonsofbitches, dirty bastards and then sonsofbitches again. They taunted the Mexicans with high cattle yells, killing them with unerring aim, then calling upon the survivors to come in and get them.

All this was not calculated to improve the red rage of the soldiers, who could walk from one end of the plaza to the other on the bodies of their dead.

The fury of the Mexicans was only whetted. North Americans were still alive in the Alamo. The bands were moving closer and the *deguello* came louder and louder, crying its ancient call for the blood of those who had made the army suffer so terribly.

Horrible were the losses of the soldiers. Blood and brains were spattered on the walls. Piles of dead everywhere a North American had made his stand. Wounded trapped under the pile of twisted bodies at the breach moaned and wriggled and tried to crawl from beneath the weight upon them.

Of the eight hundred men of the brave Toluca Battalion that had taken the shock against the north defenses, more than six hundred were dead or dying.

No time for parley.

"Kill, kill!" wailed the *deguello*.

With his left arm broken, holding it against his stomach

151

with his right hand, Lieutenant Hernandez surveyed the scene from just inside the porte-cochere. Men were turning cannons to blast the doorway of the church.

He walked over to the low wall, with Sergeant Archuleta at his heels. A soldier of the Matamoros Battalion lay across the wall, his back bent so that it hurt to look at him, his feet trapped on the other side of the wall by a tangle of dead men. A strange piece of metal extended from his smashed head.

An impulse made Hernandez pull it free. Metal shone through the gray tissue of brains clinging to it. Hernandez shook it in his hand and looked again. Bent and blackened and a thing of horror, it was nonetheless a crucifix.

Blood of Christ, a crucifix had done this thing!

Hernandez dropped it quickly and once more pulled his broken arm against his belly. Staying close to the wall, he went toward the long barracks. Behind him, Sergeant Archuleta saw the gleam of silver in the thing the lieutenant had dropped. He picked it up, looked closer, wiped it on his pants and put it into his pocket.

Rifle fire from the upper windows of the two-story barracks had driven away those across the plaza who had been trying to break in the doors of the west building. Quite evident it was to Lieutenant Hernandez that this east building must be cleaned out first.

He explained that to the sergeant, and a major nearby overheard and at once began to give orders to that effect, for which he was later given a fine decoration.

"Bring up one of those small guns—with grape," Hernandez told the sergeant.

"Yes, my lieutenant!"

"Before you do that—remove that man we saw from the wall."

Sergeant Archuleta trotted away.

Cannons were brought up. Sharpshooters standing on ladders at the west wall endeavored to keep the windows clear of riflemen, succeeding in part, although reserves who came rushing from the north, released to plunder and mutilate the dead North Americans, were thinned out painfully before they learned to hug the wall of the east barracks.

One by one the doors were broken in. Attackers rushed in, once more hurled ahead by weight behind them. Rifle and pistol fire from behind the semi-circular barricades of earth and cowhides chopped up the first onrush.

152

Then rifles and pistols were empty. The defenders died hard, backing toward the ends of the rooms, grappling with the last strength in them.

The victors dragged the bodies out, three here, five in another room, seven there. They stripped and looted them, then shot and stabbed and bayoneted some more.

On the upper floor, in the long room that was the hospital, what was left of the men of Gonzales waited.

Captain Forsyth, thirty-nine, nominally third in command of the Alamo, was now first, though he did not know that at the moment. One side of his face was shot away.

"Fill those stairs with dead men," he said, as the door below splintered and crashed.

They filled the steps with dead men, and more came lunging up over the bodies. Bit by bit the men of Gonzales were driven back toward the dark end of the room. All the candles they could find they had left burning at the front end where the steps came up.

From behind a barricade of all the furniture in the room, and the bodies of their own dead, they kept the room rolling with rifle fire, piling dead men at the landing.

"Come and get us!" someone croaked harshly, choking in the fumes of powdersmoke.

They all hurled that cry.

Gunners cleared the dead men from the steps, forty-two of them, and horsed a cannon up until its muzzle pointed along the floor. They fired it twice before the last shot came from the dark end of the room.

Then they finished up the wounded and the sick.

Billy Wells and Wilson with two others from the west wall held one of the storerooms. "I'll kneel and fire around this here end of the cowhide," Wells told Wilson. "You stand close and fire over the top."

The two men on the other end of the inner barrier took the same positions.

The door was broken down with crow bars and axes. After that there was a long moment when the only Mexicans Wells could see were those clear across the plaza by the east barracks. A group of them were carrying on their bayonets a white body that dripped red.

153

On both sides of the shattered door there was talking, and the scraping of *guaraches.*

"Come on, you murdering bastards!" Wells shouted.

They came.

He fired one pistol and then the other. Eight dead men partly blocked the doorway when the weapons in the room were empty. Wells and Wilson did not retreat. They went over the sprawled bodies with their knives, and that was a surprise move that netted them one more man each.

The powerful, broad-shouldered sergeant who drove his bayonet through Wells' body lifted him high, grunting his fury as he did, until Wells was hanging face down above the man's shoulder.

Dying, Billy Wells sank his knife in the sergeant's back.

CHAPTER 22

Now THERE WAS the chapel left. The Mexicans smashed down its doors and came in like rabid wolves. Some of the Tennesseans and others who had taken shelter there fought them to the death.

Riflemen on the firing platforms were the last strong spark of resistance. Still shooting for the head, they drilled soldiers through the crowns of their skulls. Guns empty, and time ticking out its last few seconds for them, the few who were left of the men of the Alamo hurled cannon balls, rammers, sticks and stones down on the soldiers.

And then musket balls dropped them in the long fall to the floor, or left them lying across the platforms.

Jake Walker was almost the last to die. Badly wounded, he crawled into the room where the women huddled and begged Mrs. Dickerson to write a letter to his people when she was released. A soldier shot him at her feet.

Ham had placed Jim Bowie's pistols in his hands, and his knife was on the blankets. His eyes wild with fever, at death's white door already, Bowie got the first two Mexicans through the door. He tried to lift his famous knife, but lacked the strength to do it.

The bayonets came driving.

They tossed him afterward on the long knives of the mus-

154

kets, blankets trailing from him, blood streaming down on the hands and arms and the faces of the screaming mob that bore him.

A Mexican officer, sickened by the carnage on both sides, stopped them and made them throw the body on the ground.

No woman or child in the chapel was harmed. A slender young officer spoke to the group of women. "Is a Mrs. Dickerson here?"

She hesitated, her child hard-clasped, thinking of the moment just before the chapel doors were closed, when her husband had run in and cried, "My God, Sue, the Mexicans are inside our walls! If you live, take care of the child!" And then he had plunged outside again.

"Hurry!" the officer said. "There isn't much time."

She stepped forward. "I am Mrs. Dickerson."

"Then follow me."

The officer spoke harshly to three soldiers who started to seize her when she moved. They fell back.

She tried not to see the horror of the courtyard when she followed the officer outside. She was afraid she would see her husband, looking as some of the other defenders looked.

She recognized Colonel Crockett, his fur cap near his head, a grin of hellish contentment on his long face.

The *deguello* had ceased, but some of those who had not been through the bloodiest part of the fight were still screaming and firing wildly into corpses.

A stray ball tore through the right calf of Mrs. Dickerson's leg. She cried out, faltering. The officer looked back inquiringly.

"I'm all right," she said. Holding Angelina tightly, she walked out of the Alamo.

It was after that that Santa Anna, who had started once and turned back when rifle bullets whispered past his head, rode again toward the fort to view the scene.

No longer with any duty immediately before them, the cavalry was at loose ends. Many of the officers had left their horses and walked toward the Alamo. Panfilio Olid, charged with watching their mounts, took a chance and rode up a little to see if he could peer inside the fort.

He looked back with guilt when he heard a horse running behind him. His eyes popped.

It was Veedor Bustamente, who had somehow dragged himself into the saddle. He had a lance. Like a shriveled gnome

155

to the horse he clung, riding for a few moments as of old, riding straight toward the backs of the little group with Santa Anna.

One instant Panfilio hesitated, with a wildness running in his brain, but he knew who was responsible for the fact that Veedor had been able to steal a loose horse.

Panfilio spurred his own mount hard, angling to intercept Don Bustamente. At a gallop he caught the bridle and hauled the ancient lancer's horse around.

It was too much for Veedor's old knees to hold in the violent turn. He flew to the ground, struck hard, and did not move.

Panfilio leaped down and ran to him. Don Bustamente's eyes were far away and he did not know his old friend. "I lanced a pig," he murmured, and died content.

So great was his hatred, so determined his effort, that he died actually thinking that he had lanced the pig, Panfilio thought. It was good.

A colonel came trotting over, full of frowning and great importance. "What passes here?" he demanded.

"This old one, my colonel, so great was his hatred of the North Americans—"

Bernal came running up, bumping against Panfilio in his haste. His face crumpled when he saw Veedor, and then, in anger, he shouted, "He came to kill—"

Panfilio's big hand was around his face, leaving only his eyes above it. Panfilio caught him up, holding him.

"As I was saying, and as this little one was saying, my colonel, so great was his hatred of North Americans that he came to kill one. He was a brave soldier, and he—".

"He was a great fool," the colonel snorted, and walked away.

Panfilio put Bernal down. "A big mouth is a terrible thing, little boy. You came very close to getting Panfilio Olid killed for his carelessness in allowing Don Bustamente to get a horse."

Bernal knelt beside the body.

"You are of Don Bustamente's family?"

The boy nodded.

"I will put him on a horse and—"

"I brought him here on a burro."

"Then get it," Panfilio said. He took a great, deep breath, looking down at his old comrade. No man of Don Bustamente's

156

age had ever died with such greatness, riding a lancer's horse, on his way to a great deed; and although the great deed had not come about, Don Bustamente had died believing it was so.

When Bernal, weeping now, started to lead the burro away, Panfilio put his hand on the boy's shoulder. "I say this, boy, he was the best of all the great ones."

And then Panfilio was weeping too.

El Presidente picked his way across the plaza. His face was white with anger. Pigs! These North American pigs, so few in number, had done this to *him*.

He knew full well that many of his men would desert before they would follow him on to scourge Texas with blood and fire. They would be afraid to fight again men like these of the Alamo. These pigs who lay white and lifeless were but few compared to the bodies of the soldiers they had killed.

A great army had been crippled. Already, all around the outside of the fort, the cursed women who had followed their men on the long march were screaming and moaning as they found their dead. And soon they would have to be let inside the Alamo.

Crippled though the army was, it would go on, and the blood of rebels, foreigners, pigs would flow deep all over the colonies for this outrage.

The lust had died from the soldiers' eyes. They were washed with blood and now it was revolting them. They found the last live man in the Alamo, William Linn, who had been a gunner on the eighteen-pounder.

He had been shot twice when the others fell dead around him after the last lethal crash of the big gun, but he had staggered into a storeroom on the south wall and hidden among moldy mattresses.

Now they had dragged him out, and they didn't want to kill him.

Lieutenant Hernandez, faint from loss of blood and pain, led the men that hauled Linn before El Presidente.

"Your Excellency," he said, swaying on his feet, "this one was found by some of my men. I thought he might be spared, if your Excellency—"

"You thought!" Santa Anna's face turned even whiter with fury. "You will not be a lieutenant long if you cannot remember orders! You know them?"

"Yes, your Excellency," Hernandez said.

157

Hernandez looked at Sergeant Archuleta.

The muskets crashed as the soldiers stepped away from Linn.

March 6, 1836, on a Sunday, about 9:00 A.M.

The last man of the Alamo was dead.

AND AFTERWARD

THEY BURNED the bodies of the men of the Alamo, a layer of wood, a layer of dead men, more wood, more corpses. It was the greatest insult Santa Anna could devise. Where the bodies were burned no one can say, for all accounts are contradictory.

One man of the garrison was not destroyed by fire. The family of Gregorio Esparza was allowed to take his body away after pleading with Santa Anna.

Later, some of the ashes of the funeral pyres were buried by men of the Texas army. Again, no one can say where with certainty.

Some of the Mexican dead were buried. Most of them were thrown into the San Antonio River by the over-taxed citizens who had no more room in their cemetery. Once more accounts vary widely, but that sixteen hundred soldiers died in taking the Alamo, or of wounds afterward, is probably conservative. By eye-witness account, such surgeons as the Mexican army had could not have diagnosed or treated a hangnail.

All the women and children who had suffered through the siege inside the Alamo were released unharmed, as was Joe, Travis' servant. Mrs. Dickerson and her child were treated kindly, given a horse by Santa Anna, put in charge of Ben, Santa Anna's Negro servant, and sent to Gonzales.

On the way they overtook Joe, who had escaped by himself from Santa Anna's hospitality.

Shattered by their victory, the Mexicans had to rebuild their army. Meanwhile, General Urrea had gobbled up stragglers of the abortive Matamoros expedition at San Patricio and at Agua Dulce Creek. Then his dragoons captured Colonel Fannin's four hundred and fifty men on open ground near Goliad.

Why had not Fannin gone to the relief of the Alamo long before that? That is difficult to explain. He actually did make

158

a start once, went a few miles, and then a wagon broke down. His officers called for a council. Some of the oxen strayed. The council voted to go back to the fort at Goliad, and that they did.

When Fannin's command was captured later, after a skirmish, they had halted in an indefensible position because of another broken wagon. General Urrea granted them an honorable surrender. They were promised parole.

By direct orders of Santa Anna, on March 27, 1836, another Sunday, Fannin's men were marched out and three hundred and ninety of them were shot in cold blood. "Detestable delinquents," Santa Anna called them, in rebuking General Urrea for not having murdered them as soon as captured.

The men of the Alamo had supplied the time that Texans needed. Both the Alamo and Goliad gave Texas unity through rage, and a famous war cry to hang the unity on.

Santa Anna knew the Latin mind as few men ever did, but he certainly did not understand the minds of North Americans.

Recruited, his army somewhat restored, he finally left the stench of Bexar, as indeed did all the citizens of the place when the stink became unspeakable. Santa Anna resumed his march into Texas to deal with all the rest of the "detestable delinquents."

Southern Texas ran before him in what has been termed the great "Runaway Scrape." And old Sam Houston with the army he had raised kept running too. He fell back from the Colorado, from the Brazos—and he kept falling back, and all the while his army grew more mutinous because old Sam wouldn't make a stand and give them a chance to avenge the Alamo and Goliad.

Day by day Texans deserted Sam Houston and went to protect their families in the Runaway Scrape.

Still, he retreated, and his tight, slash mouth confided nothing to officers or men, who were almost as mad at Sam Houston by then as they were at Santa Anna.

At last he found a place to his liking, whether by accident or design no man knows. He burned the one bridge by which he could have retreated. Near a bend in the San Jacinto River, April 21, 1836, the Texas army in one hell-roaring charge slaughtered a superior force under El Presidente in person.

They plucked Santa Anna out of the weeds the next day, where he was scrabbling along in terror, wearing filthy clothes he had found in a deserted shack. Suggestions for disposing of him ranged from Apache skull-roasting over a slow fire to nailing his testicles to a stump and pushing him over backward.

To Houston's everlasting credit, Santa Anna was protected. U.S. President Andrew Jackson, in a letter of September 4, 1836, advised Houston: ". . . let not his blood be shed unless it becomes necessary by an imperative act of just retaliation of Mexican massacres hereafter. This is what I think true wisdom and humanity dictates . . ."

Santa Anna eventually went back to Mexico unharmed. Promptly he disavowed all promises he had made as a prisoner as not binding on the Supreme Government of Mexico, namely, himself.

He was one dictator of a Latin country who didn't die suddenly of lead poisoning. Shrewd as a rat, with a keen insight of Mexican character, he continued to skim through the politics of Mexico like a bat through a wire maze, several times in and out of absolute control of the country until 1855. His final attempt at a coup-d'état failed in 1867. He died unregretted and in poverty in Mexico City, June 21, 1876.

All memoirs must be read with extreme reservation, but Santa Anna's memoirs take the rag right off the bush when it comes to downright lying, including the statement that he "buried six hundred foreigners in the ditches" after the Alamo fell.

But, as a leading Mexican newspaper said, giving one scant paragraph to his obituary, "Peace to his ashes."

So ought it be.

And greater peace to the ashes of the Men of the Alamo . . .